Life is Not a Bed of Roses

A Second Set of Short Stories

by

Elizabeth Ducie and Sharon Cook

Chudleigh Phoenix Publications

A Chudleigh Phoenix Publications book

Copyright ©: Elizabeth Ducie and Sharon Cook 2012

Illustration by Colin Avery

All rights reserved.

No part of this publication may be reproduced, stored in a retrieval system, or transmitted, in any form or by any means, without the prior permission in writing of the publisher, nor be otherwise circulated in any form of binding or cover other than that in which it is published and without a similar condition including this condition being imposed on the subsequent purchaser.

ISBN: 978-0-9569508-2-6

Printed by Hedgerow Print, Crediton, Devon EX17 1ES

Chudleigh Phoenix Publications
A Division of
Heathside Information Services Ltd

Contents

The Apprentice	1
Five Oranges	5
The Well Brought-Up Woman	11
Just One More Ball	17
Devon Time	28
One Too Many	42
The Stories of Pavel and Yuri	47
Tale of Two Gardens	53
Business as Usual	63
The Outcasts	76

About the Authors

Elizabeth Ducie has given up her secret life as an international jet-setter and now writes full-time when she's not editing the Chudleigh Phoenix Community Magazine; working on her author 'platform'; or throwing herself with gusto into the life of the small Devon town she now calls home. She's looking forward to the invention of the thirty-six hour day.

Sharon Cook skidded to a halt in Devon almost five years ago, with two young children in tow. From their seventeenth-century cottage, she is fulfilling a dream of the five-year-old she once was and, when not avoiding housework, she writes. Building on 20 years experience as a journalist and food writer, Sharon remains utterly fascinated by people. Making quilts and chutney keeps her sane… sometimes.

***

Sharon says: This book is dedicated to Harrison and Poppy, who are wonderful — even when they aren't; and to Alex, of course. And all writing friends out there who listened, encouraged and believed, especially Jackie.

Elizabeth says: To Michael — as always.

For more information about the authors or about Chudleigh Phoenix Publications, visit our website at www.chudleighphoenix.co.uk

The Apprentice
Elizabeth Ducie

"I think it may be time to hand over the reins," Henry said, kissing Claire's picture and switching out the light. "Goodnight, old girl."

Henry Ross was tired. Not just bone tired from shifting furniture around all day, but world-weary. He'd tried so hard to keep the junk shop going after his wife died, but there's no fun in discovering a hidden gem when you've no-one to share it with. He wasn't sure he could be bothered any longer.

Timothy Snelling was employed as Henry's assistant in the shop. A tall boy who tended to stoop to disguise his height, he'd left school two years before with an undistinguished academic record. Despite numerous applications and a handful of interviews, he'd not managed to find a job in the following three months. His mother, an old friend of Claire's, had brought him in to see Henry when she got fed up with him sitting watching daytime TV.

"Timothy, I'm thinking of taking things easier in the future, maybe only coming in three days a week," Henry said, next day. "I'm going to need a part-time shop manager. Are you interested?"

"I guess so," Timothy murmured uncertainly, flushing hotly. "Would I have to go on a training course?"

"Not necessarily," said Henry, "I could train you myself. What we'll do is keep a record of what you sell over the next few weeks and you can show me everything you've learnt about the job. Then, we'll see if you're ready."

"OK boss," the boy replied, "I'll give it a go." But it didn't sound to Henry like he was that keen on the idea.

Two weeks later, Henry was cataloguing some new stock when the shop-bell rang. A slim red-haired girl in her late teens strode up to the counter. She looked vaguely familiar, but Henry couldn't put a name to the face.

"I'm Rosie Yates," she said, holding her hand out confidentially to Timothy who was leaning against the counter, staring into space. "I've got some stuff you might be interested in buying." He looked around uncertainly, but Henry waved at him to carry on. This was a chance to see what the boy could do. Rosie tipped a pile of jewellery onto the counter.

"It belongs to my Gran, but she doesn't wear it anymore."

Timothy sorted through the pile.

"Three pearl necklaces, seven brooches including a couple of cameos, and a pair of emerald ear-rings. Hundred quid for the lot," he said.

"Is that all?" she sighed. "I was hoping for double."

"OK, how's about I meet you half-way? One fifty."

"Done." The girl put out her hand again and pumped Timothy's hand up and down with a big smile on her face. "Gran's putting it towards a new telly."

After she'd gone, Timothy carried the new stock over to Henry.

"I reckon we'll at least double our money on this lot," he crowed.

"Oh Timothy, she saw you coming," grinned Henry, shaking his head. "The pearls are fakes, cameos aren't selling at all these days — and the emeralds look suspiciously like glass to me. We'll be lucky to break even."

Two weeks later, Henry was sitting in the café over the road, sipping his morning coffee, when he saw Rosie entering the shop again. Once again, he was sure he knew her from somewhere.

The girl prowled around for a while, and then stopped in front of a pile of old suitcases. Henry saw her call Timothy over. After a short discussion, she shook his hand and took some money from her purse. Picking up the smallest case, she strolled towards the door. With her hand on the door handle, she stopped and said something else. Pulling another note from her purse she swapped it for a small item that she pushed into her handbag. As she walked down the street, Henry could see she was grinning broadly.

"Henry, you'll never guess what happened," Timothy said when his boss returned to the shop. "That red-head came back and I've just sold her an old leather suitcase — for forty quid! The one you said we'd never shift."

"Forty quid — are you sure?" Henry replied.

"Yes. She was going to pay thirty but then offered another ten if I threw in one of those little vases you bought yesterday. She said it was just like one her Gran used to have."

"What did it look like?" Henry asked quietly.

"It was the pale pink glass one — all cloudy-like." Timothy was still grinning over his sale. "You said it might be French."

"Not the one I thought was a Lalique?" Henry cried. "Oh Timothy, how could you?"

The vase hadn't cost him that much, it was part of a job lot. But this was the second time the girl had got the better of his apprentice.

"I'm not getting the job, am I Henry?" Timothy said with relief in his voice.

"No, lad," Henry replied. "I don't think you are. Did you get Rosie's address by any chance?"

"Yes," said Timothy "why?"

"Well," Henry said, starting to laugh and glancing at the picture of the red-haired elderly woman sitting on his desk, "I've just realised who she reminds me of. I think I might give her a ring and have a chat — and see if she wants a job."

Five Oranges
Sharon Cook

It was no surprise when the 'Brenda and Marcia' show came to a shuddering halt one day, over five oranges. Well, actually, it was five oranges, four apples, three bananas, two luxury Fruit and Nut bars and a copy of The Telegraph. Having worked in the small and most imperfectly formed hospital shop for more than six years, Marcia was still shocked when it came to an end.

She had seen so much, heard so many life stories, witnessed so much pain, and suffering and joy. From the birth and death of babies to the healing of limbs, the highs and lows of the cancer patients and their families, confusing diagnoses, time wasters, worriers, bores and no end of dramas and love stories — mostly played out by hospital staff. Sick children were always hard. Accident victims both shocking and touching. Some people found religion; others seemed to have too much. Some had far too much emotion, others not enough.

Having lived such a straightforward, uncomplicated life herself Marcia was always calm and adept at handling all comers. All her life she had lived in the same town, known the same people and been comforted by the same friends when her beloved Alfred passed on at just 62.

He had suffered a massive stroke, and she watched as the ambulance crew — a lively duo whom she now knew as regular chocolate purchasers ever since she had started at the shop — bought him back to life on their front driveway before rushing him in to the hospital. Sadly, the stroke had been too much and Alfred was buried just over six years ago. Three months later her grief had taken her to work in the hospital shop. It had become a reason for getting up; and so friendly and helpful had she become that, in time, she was actually paid a small wage as 'assistant manager' to the imposing Brenda.

How could five oranges have led to the end, thought Marcia sadly? The little shop meant so much to her.

The end had been brought about by Brenda. Bossy (some might describe her as a bit of a control freak), efficient, not very good at listening to others and with a life utterly dominated by the seething resentment, evident to far too many, for her daughter-in-law.

"Why that woman had to go and marry 'my Brian' I don't know," was a common Brenda refrain. "He could have had his pick of umpteen women. She's not even got a degree, unlike 'my Brian'. Of course he got a 2:2 from Plymouth University." On and on, Marcia knew it all — as did anyone who stood still long enough to be talked at. "He has to do all the cooking, you know, she's too busy working. And he does the hoovering. I mean, what does she do with her time apart from work and ferry the children about in her expensive car?"

Always immaculately groomed, Brenda ran the shop with a rod of iron. It made quite a decent profit, with all proceeds going to the ward which attracted most cheque presentations and local media coverage, the premature baby unit.

While Marcia and Brenda were both widows and both in their mid-60s, that is where the commonality ended. Well, they both liked Crunchies, but that didn't really count. Brenda was doom to Marcia's charm.

Brenda was deaf to the language of others, so weighed down by moaning about her daughter-in-law, she never had much time to visit her other two grandchildren. It meant driving to another town, swallowing her shame over her daughter's divorce and admitting to her 'friends' — the bridge circle who still tolerated her and the church congregation who had little choice — that her only other child was a 'single parent'.

Marcia soothed customers, Brenda irritated them. People talked to Marcia, regulars tried to avoid Brenda.

***

Marcia was running the shop when the phone rang on Christmas Eve. A well-spoken man asked if she could put together a little package for his brother, who had had the misfortune to hit a tree while travelling at fifty miles an hour. He had broken both his legs and too many ribs to fit on a single X-ray.

"I'm so sorry," said Marcia, "we don't actually take credit cards."

"Oh no!" said the man, "I'm calling from Austria and I can't get to see my brother — is there any way around this?" Pausing for a few seconds, Marcia thought 'it's Christmas, why not?'

"Look," said the kindly pensioner, "can you send me a cheque? I shouldn't, but I'm sure you can be trusted," Marcia chuckled. She'd not got it wrong once in all her time in the shop. Some people you can trust, others you just knew not to go there. It was, however, breaking all Brenda's rules: "No tic. No credit. No IOUs under any circumstances."

The deal was struck and Marcia parcelled up a delightful fruit basket (with a few extras thrown in) and had it sent to the relevant ward. The recipient, a solicitor in his early 40s, was greatly touched by his brother's gesture, particularly as they hadn't spoken for two years following a disagreement over a girlfriend's dog and a bowl of sardines. He was never to know his accident also changed the course of two women's lives.

Marcia's gesture was not well received by Brenda. When she found, on Boxing Day, the note in the till from Marcia (along with a Christmas card and a rather nice box of chocolates from her caring colleague) she was so incensed she grabbed the phone to have it out with Marcia. The tirade which followed was heard by at least three customers — an eminent eye surgeon and two midwives.

The words "gross insubordination...giving away the profits...stupidity of the highest order...idiot woman... Marcia, you're fired" rang around the shop. It was quite unpleasant.

Mr Sirius Templeman was horrified. He had a soft spot for Marcia; she always saved him the ripest bananas and refused to charge him, saying they were almost past their sell-by date. It was about time this miserable woman manager, who only ever moaned, was taken down a peg or two. He'd have a word with the Board...

"And a Merry Christmas to you, Brenda," he smiled, as she overcharged him for a bunch of far too unripe bananas and a copy of The Times.

Marcia had a very quiet Christmas. She and Alfred had been unable to have children, but she always shared turkey and Christmas pud with her sister and whichever of her children were visiting that year. There was also the dog to walk, a neighbour or two to help out and a good old New Year's Eve knees-up to look forward to at the day centre where she helped out on Sundays.

The shock Marcia had felt at the phone call from Brenda was totally offset, a few days later, by a call from one of the county's top eye surgeons, who just happened to be a lover of very ripe bananas.

Marcia tried desperately hard not to feel too smug about this second phone call. Smug was not good, but never once had Marcia ever moaned about Brenda and her relenting unpleasantness. Alfred had always said 'what goes around comes around, girl'. It seemed that, yet again, he had been right.

While doing the rounds of the festive drinks parties, Mr Templeman had spoken to quite a few of the hospital 'glitterati', most of who had been pretty well oiled when they talked. For some years, there had been talk of a second hospital shop, right at the front of the hospital's brand spanking new entrance. The time had come to forge ahead, particularly in light of a rather grand gesture from the relative of a recent patient.

Among the post which arrived between Christmas and the New Year was a card from an eminent Austrian businessman, depicting a snow-covered Schönbrunn Palace. Inside nestled a cheque for £50,000, plus the money for a special fruit basket. The donation, explained the touching letter inside, was to say thank you for the kindness and trust shown to him when he had rung the hospital shop following his brother's accident.

***

By the time Marcia was installed as the manager in the new shop, on a decent salary which would at least enable her to have a holiday each year, Brenda was apoplectic with rage. How dare Marcia be promoted over her? How dare the hospital board believe Marcia would be better at running the lovely new shop? Life was so unfair. It was wrong, it should not be allowed.

"What experience does she have for goodness sake?" she would demand of regular customers. "She'll give away all the profits, then how will we be able to present any cheques. Mark my words, that charity will suffer!" she droned on. Brenda's tirade went on for months. She ranted at whoever would listen, even her daughter-in-law. Gradually the customers passing through the old shop dropped right off. Even the staff who worked in the wards right next to it preferred to walk to the other side of the sprawling hospital, just to escape Brenda's unpleasantness.

By the summer meeting of the hospital board's steering committee it was decided to close down the old shop, and concentrate on promoting the new one. Sad to lose staff, agreed the board, but the new, larger shop could possibly absorb all the volunteers. The only victim of the cut could, it was agreed, perhaps be offered some part-time hours. A motion was put forward, by Sirius Templeman, to ask Marcia if she would be able to find a place for Brenda.

Smiling quietly to himself, he was heard to say: "I'm sure the very capable Marcia will know exactly how to handle such an appointment."

The Well Brought-up Woman
Elizabeth Ducie

"I'll have these, please," said Felicity, handing the Sabatier knives to the elderly shop assistant. "They're expensive, but it's an investment. My tutor recommended we buy the best we can afford." Having spent a good portion of her weekly allowance in one go, she took the parcel and smiled at the assistant. "Thank you very much. Have a good weekend."

"What a nice young woman, and such excellent manners," said the assistant to his manager as they watched her leave the shop. "Not like most of the other young people we get in here these days."

***

Felicity's such a good girl, what wonderful manners. She'd heard that sentence throughout her childhood. It was small reward for the hard work she'd put in. All her memories, from her earliest days, were of her mother scolding her.

Sit still, don't fidget. That was hard for a toddler, eager to explore her surroundings and get on with playing. Every time her parents' friends came to visit, she would sit for hours, trying not to wriggle.

Be quiet, you can't talk in here. She'd been frightened in the dark, echoing church, where an old man shouted at them from the altar. They'd all knelt and prayed for forgiveness, overlooked by larger than life statues of saints and saviours. So she'd asked her mother if they were all going to hell. All she'd wanted was a little reassurance, not a silent pinch that bruised her leg for days afterwards.

Little girls should be seen and not heard. That was the day she'd tried to join in the adult conversation when they'd met a neighbour during a shopping trip. At the time, her mother had hissed that one sentence at her, before turning with a smile to continue talking. Later she'd smacked Felicity hard across the face and sent her to bed with no supper.

Don't talk with your mouth full. The day she'd got a gold star at school for reading, she'd been so excited. Her father had come home from work as she was eating her tea and she'd rushed into telling him the news without waiting to swallow. Her mother had brought a hand down hard on the table and then made Felicity finish her meal in silence. After that, the gold star didn't seem quite as shiny.

Where did you get that gum from? Spit it out now! Nice girls don't chew gum! She was twelve and had just moved to 'big school'. Her new friend Hannah had given her the gum as they walked out of the school gates and they had been practising blowing bubbles. Felicity hadn't noticed her mother walking towards them until it was too late. As she was frog-marched down the street, she'd looked back over her shoulder. Hannah had crossed over to meet another group of friends — and they were all sniggering in her direction.

Of course you can't go out tonight. You've got school in the morning. Besides, I don't want you mixing with that crowd. They have no idea how to behave, must have been dragged up! She'd been shopping with her mother when they bumped into a group of old friends from primary school days. They'd lost touch when she'd gone to the grammar school and they to the local comprehensive. Their paths had rarely crossed since but they seemed pleased to see her and eagerly pressed her to join them at a gig that night. Her mother had smiled politely and said nothing until they got home. Then she'd refused point-blank to consider letting Felicity go.

She's a credit to you; such a hard worker and always does what she's told. You must be very proud of her. Every Parents' Evening it had been the same story. Felicity had worked hard, was never late handing in homework and got straight 'A' grades at both GCSE and A-level.

What a shame you won't be able to get home very often. Her parents' friends were surprised when Felicity applied to study history at the University of St Andrews, such a long way from Devon. However, no one was surprised when she was accepted. They all knew she would succeed wherever she went. They just thought it was such a pity she would find it too expensive and time-consuming to get home more than once a term.

***

Felicity found it very strange at first, living on her own, with no parental guidance. Realising that no one shouted if she didn't do all her preparation work was an eye-opener. It was an even bigger surprise that no one seemed to care too much if she didn't hand in her seminar assignments.

During her first week, she signed up for all sorts of clubs and societies. At Freshers' Fair, everyone was trying so hard to make the newcomers feel welcome. Each time she made eye-contact with one of the eager students manning the stalls, they'd engage her in conversation which would always end the same way.

Do sign up and come along to our first meeting... our first get-together... our first event... It would have been rude to walk away. So she signed. Soon her pigeon-hole was full of flyers, leaflets and invites. Her inbox received messages daily. Her self-imposed rule, to only go out at weekends, was broken by week three and by the mid-term reading week, she was out every night, and several times on Saturdays and Sundays.

Dutifully, but without anticipation, she returned to her parents for Christmas. She knew there would be little else to do except study, so she took a pile of books with her. But the previous lack of work showed and she was unable to catch up in time.

Most of her marks for the January exams barely skated above a pass and she recorded her first ever 'fail' in the module on the American Civil War. The day after the results were posted, her tutor took her to one side and told her he was worried about her ability to stay on the course.

It was at this crucial time that she met Edward. He was a post-graduate economist, with an apartment on the edge of town. Three weeks later, she left her place in Hall and moved in with him. He was quiet, studious and polite.

That's not how well-brought-up girls behave. She just knew that would be her mother's reaction, so she didn't tell her parents about her new living arrangements.

Felicity and Edward quickly settled into a routine. Every evening he would read items from the newspaper to her while she cooked their evening meal. She wasn't a great cook, but pasta and cook-in sauces were what Edward liked too, so they were both happy. Later, they would sit on opposite sides of the room reading or writing, occasionally exchanging smiles if they happened to look up at the same time.

She resigned from all the clubs and societies. She stopped going out on week-nights. All her preparation was up to date; her assignments handed in on time. She started getting top marks in her examinations and her tutor stopped worrying about her. Classmates commented on the change from the wild party-goer of the previous term. They didn't realise they were seeing the real Felicity for the first time.

***

Four years later, Felicity gained a First Class Honours degree in history and stayed on at St Andrews to study for a Masters. Edward had finished his Doctorate and was now working as advisor to the Managing Director of a large marketing company. He talked about the experience being *good for his CV* and occasionally suggested he might move into politics in the future. He asked her to marry him, and she accepted without a moment's hesitation. It was a quiet wedding. Her parents were invited, but didn't attend because *the travel would be too much for your father.* They moved into a two-bedded, semi-detached house in the suburbs and quickly settled into married life.

One evening, Edward invited the boss and his wife to dinner. Felicity was late home and had to rush to get the food ready on time. It was not perfect by any means — the meat was tough and the vegetables were on the crunchy side of *al dente.* Edward said nothing until the guests had gone.

"That's not how I expect our guests to be treated," he said. "You'll need to improve your cooking skills. We'll be entertaining quite a bit from now on."

Felicity enrolled at a local cookery school and bought her chef's knives. She tried. She really tried. But something always went wrong. Either the meal was underdone and too chewy or it was overdone and charred. Edward would try each dish and then look at her sadly, shaking his head.

"I don't understand it," he said after she'd been on the course for several weeks. "All well brought-up women should be able to cook properly. Why can't you?"

Felicity picked up the largest of the knives from her set, walked calmly across the kitchen and plunged the blade into her husband's neck. Afterwards, she smiled at the body slumped across the table.

"Thank you so much for having me," she said, "I've had a wonderful time, but I really must be leaving. I need to go home now." Then packing her knives carefully in the boot of her car, she started the long journey south. There was something she'd been meaning to say to her mother for years — and it couldn't wait any longer.

Just One More Ball
Sharon Cook

It wasn't that Cynthia was bored. Far from it. There was always plenty to do. Looking after Gerald had been her main priority for several decades. Teenage sweethearts, the pair had married in the 1960s, had a son and a daughter, worked hard and created a beautiful home with a well-kept garden. With four grandchildren scattered across the country, two foreign holidays and a trip to Scotland each year, their diary was always pretty lively.

Now retired, Gerald had gone from accountant to golf player in one easy swing. Cynthia was well regarded in their small, rural town and both of them played their part in all the required community happenings. Oh yes, they were quite 'comfortable', in every sense of the word. Cynthia had a nice life. An unremarkable life. A quiet life.

But Cynthia felt unsettled. She had just finished clearing up after a coffee morning fundraising for the local donkey sanctuary — one of the many and varied charities which she and Gerald had supported over the years — when it dawned on her. Never, in all her 66 years, had she ever really had a proper 'adventure'.

The more Cynthia thought, the more she realised her whole life had been spent in the 'safe lane'. It had all been very pleasant. She had no complaints. Life with Gerald was constant, and safe, and had bought its own rewards. Both her children were happy and settled and her family had never been troubled by illness other than the routine. No one had ever broken a bone, had a car accident, spent a night in hospital, or received life-saving treatment.

The more she thought, the more she began to realise just how lucky her family had been. As a regular church goer, Cynthia often said a silent prayer of thanks for all the good things her family had in life.

By the time Gerald came home from the golf club to cottage pie and runner beans — from their own garden — Cynthia was in quite a state.

"What on earth is the matter with you?" he enquired, pouring them both a second glass of Croft Original.

"I'm not really sure," replied his flustered wife.

"Well come on girl, spit it out," laughed Gerald.

"But that's just it, I don't really know." Sipping her sherry as she dished out the dinner, Cynthia then joined her husband at their polished, dark wood dining room table, and began forking the home-cooked favourite into her mouth.

"Gerald?"

"Yes dear," replied the bemused spouse, cautiously.

"Do you ever wonder why we're here? Do you ever think about what our lives might have been like if you had worked abroad — or we hadn't had Emily and Trevor? Or if you'd ever lost your job?"

Somewhat irritated by his wife's musings — dinner was always so much more pleasant when he could talk about that day's golf game and how he'd beaten that rather pompous town councillor, or how he'd managed to get out of the tricky bunker with just one shot — Gerald appeased his wife with the old: "I'm just happy to be with you, my sweet. Now what's for pudding?" Still deep in thought Cynthia served up lemon posset and put the kettle on.

"Devil of a job with the golf trolley today," opined Gerald. "I think the wheel's had it. I'll have to go into town tomorrow and start looking for a new one."

As Gerald flicked through that day's Telegraph Cynthia washed up. 'I wonder,' she thought, 'what would an adventure feel like?'

***

The following morning Cynthia had just enough time to clean the living room before heading out for a committee meeting at the church. Putting her knitting to one side, she picked up yesterday's paper and, just as she was about to put it in the recycling bin, she noticed an intriguing headline. Turning to an inside page, Cynthia found herself looking at a small car which had been entirely covered in knitting. It was quite incredible. All those little knitted squares sewn together to cover the body work, while the bumper had its own cover and there were even knitted bits on the windscreen wipers. Contrasting stripy bits were carefully sewn around the wing mirrors and you could even see the door handles as some clever knitter had made special covers to contrast with the rest of the car.

It was beautiful. The work was stunning. Utterly intrigued, Cynthia, an avid knitter herself, began to read about the 'quiet revolution' gripping knitting communities right across the world. Lamp posts, fences, parking meters, abandoned bikes, railings, unused bins, statues, even trees and a garden shed. Anything which could be covered in wool — either by knitting or crochet

— was being targeted by international yarn guerrillas. 'Knit graffiti' was appearing all over the world.

One unnamed knitter was quoted as saying: "We donate our work to public spaces. We don't just want to make people smile; we want everyone to know just how great knitting and crochet are." The craft expert quoted described the phenomenon as 'yarn bombing', adding it was widely becoming seen as a legitimate form of covert textile street art.

By the time Cynthia arrived at the committee meeting to discuss flower rotas, she felt quite flushed. She couldn't stop thinking 'what if?'

***

After chicken casserole and apple crumble that night Cynthia set about the plan slowly forming in her head. As far back as she could remember, Cynthia had been a knitter. It all came from her grandmother, who had kept whole regiments in World War II kitted out with warm woollen socks. Cynthia had spent so many hours with her grandmother, winding wool, unpicking old jumpers and sewing up newly-knitted cardigans, that she had been able to knit virtually in her sleep by the time she was twelve years old. As she got older her friends had asked her to knit clothes for them and she had amassed a huge number of patterns, half-used balls of wool and expertise.

Over the years her children had happily worn unique hand-knitted jumpers, then refused by the time they were teenagers. When hand-knitted and vintage became fashionable, Cynthia couldn't keep up with demand and regular packages of hand-knitted goodies were parcelled up and sent off to family and grateful friends. Gerald's wardrobe had various Christmas jumpers stashed away, each documenting another year lived. He particularly liked the woollen golf-inspired creations, especially the socks, which kept him warm out on the course.

Cynthia had won prizes at the WI for her knitting and had even created a knitted nativity for the church, which had been gracing one of the deep window sills — a prime position — for the last 25 years. Blankets, scarves, gloves, hats; even a knitted cloak for a grandson to wear to a Halloween party. Cynthia drew the line at knitted toilet roll holders, but a fair few teapots had been graced with one of her more quirky designs.

Having resisted the 'stitch and bitch' group, which met every Thursday afternoon at the back of the library — mostly young mums talking about toddlers — Cynthia had, at one point, joined a 'knit and natter' gathering at the town hall, which met every other Tuesday evening. But it hadn't felt quite right. Mrs Delaney from the Post Office talked over everyone and the home-made biscuits from Mrs Fancy were always inedible — so she had opted out.

Maybe, figured Cynthia, her time had come. After a quick rummage in the spare room, she dug out some of her unfinished projects. She placed a stripy scarf, abandoned because the colours hadn't quite worked, inside a cloth bag alongside some spare wool, a large needle and pair of scissors.

Later that evening, Cynthia told Gerald she was just popping out to drop off a book. Walking under cover of darkness to the small park round the corner Cynthia, very aware of all the local dog walkers, boldly walked up to the large silver birch and wrapped the scarf — lengthways — around the narrow trunk and swiftly whip stitched the two sides together. Snipping off the ends she stood back, and gasped. It looked wonderful. The light and dark greens, laced with shimmering off-white glittery wool, looked stunning on the tree.

'Must dash,' she thought, 'I don't want to get caught.' Giggling to herself all the way home she opened the front door and shouted through to Gerald: "Fancy a cuppa, dear?"

Apparently gripped by a golf DVD, Gerald didn't notice his wife's flushed face, didn't clock her racing pulse or see the glow of excitement infusing her entire visage. As they sat in their respective armchairs watching the 10 o'clock news, Cynthia's mind was on fire.

***

It took three days before anyone actually noticed the silver birch scarf.

"Pretty mummy" said a small passing boy.

"Have you seen…?" mums started chattering in the park. "I wonder who…?" they continued.

By the time a forest of crocheted flowers appeared on the chain link fence by the paper shop, Cynthia had braved the internet and was finding all sorts of ideas. It took her three weeks to knit a telephone box cover, which she fitted at 3am to avoid detection. It was so beautifully created, the takings in the phone box actually went up, a talking point in itself. Gerald had blissfully slept through her night excursion.

By the time the three parking meters in the car park were covered, even the town council had discussed the 'yarn bombing' creeping through their town.

The 'stitch and bitchers' started talking to the 'knit and natterers', each group convinced the other was responsible, though the youngsters wondered how the oldies could achieve such dizzy heights, while conceding the knitting techniques were definitely better executed than their own. The local paper came and took pictures, which were also published on the internet.

Cynthia wondered how much longer she could keep clicking away, before she was rumbled. But each new installation gave her such a buzz, she just couldn't stop. The war memorial railings, which she adorned with bright red poppies, had almost been her downfall. Those late night dog walkers were quite a hazard.

The bus shelter down Fore Street had been her favourite to date. She'd even had to drive to a town some 50 miles away to buy more wool supplies as she didn't want to get caught out; she was having so much fun.

Gerald noticed nothing; he'd long ago stopped showing any interest in Cynthia's knitting projects. Occasionally, Cynthia had to knit a jumper for a grandchild, just to keep up appearances.

Her designs became more and more quirky. A stylish hat for a small statue of a child in the big park. A hanging basket of bright pink Busy Lizzies for the town hall entrance — almost caught by a group of teenage boys trying to be clever about smoking. An amazing sheep's head to adorn the butchers' sign and a pub notice board framed with golden stars.

One morning Cynthia was amazed to see every lamp post in her street, and the next one, had been adorned with scarves. She had competition. It spurred her on and her excitement mounted. When the motorbike, permanently parked in the car park of the flats opposite, was yarn bombed Cynthia knew she had to make contact with her rival. She decided to set a challenge.

Having finished and fitted the football-themed gate coverings for the big park, Cynthia decided to start knitting window boxes for every ground floor public window sill. Easy to install, fun to do and she really needed to start using up all the left over bits of wool.

Cynthia knew her yarn bombing would have to end soon. She wanted to retain her anonymity and, with all the publicity emerging, she needed to back off. But she was intrigued by her fellow knitter. If she left every second window sill empty, would her fellow fuzzy pick up the gauntlet?

By chance, Cynthia started walking an elderly friend's dog, and she used the unsuspecting canine as her cover. Sure enough she began to spot a young woman carrying a supermarket cloth bag, similar to her own, each time a second window box appeared. One night she struck lucky and, just as the thirty-something young woman snipped the ends off a wonderful window box stuffed full of bright red knitted zinnias, Cynthia pounced.

"I love it," proclaimed Cynthia, grinning at the shocked gloved woman.

"Er, do I know you?" flannelled the bag carrier.

"Actually, I think we know each other's work quite well," beamed Cynthia.

"Oh wow! It's you. You're brilliant. But look, let's get out of here. I don't think either of us actually wants to get caught." Safely installed in a nearby pub Cynthia and Fay drank white wine and swapped notes.

Fay was a single mum on a mission — to retain her sanity and have some fun. She was also trying to fill time away from home. Having been forced to move back in with her own mum following marriage breakdown, Fay confessed she couldn't bear her mother's new boyfriend.

"He's awful, so lecherous. They met up at the golf club and, quite frankly, seeing your mum on the sofa with an aging Lothario suctioned to her face is quite disgusting." Fay shuddered at the thought.

"Poor you," sympathised Cynthia. "Knitting is so much fun though, I get such a thrill out of it," confessed the pensioner. "I never thought I'd say it, but the buzz I get from not getting caught is quite fantastic," she added, eyes glittering. The naughty knitters agreed to meet again the following week — perhaps they could collaborate on something?

Cynthia arrived home just before Gerald: "And how was the 19th hole?" she laughed.

"Good thanks dear," he mumbled, looking momentarily bemused, before switching on the telly for the 10 o'clock news.

***

It didn't take Fay long to figure out that her mum's lover was Cynthia's husband. Gerald had quite a reputation among the 'women of a certain age' in the town. In fact,

Life Is Not a Bed of Roses

the only person who seemed not to be aware of her husbands 'golfing' prowess was Cynthia. But what was Fay to do? She adored her new friend, and the two women had had so much fun knitting a shed cover for an unused, unloved heap of wood up at the allotments. It was the talk of the town!

By then the covert textile duo had decided to end their nocturnal activities for a few months, just to ensure they didn't get caught. Except Fay had one last idea…

Having dropped out of art school as a teenager, the young mum had never quite given up some of her more creative ambitions. And it really showed in her final installation.

***

When Gerald arrived to play golf on Friday, he couldn't help but notice the crowd gathered around a stunning knitted wall-hanging hung from the outside of the golf-trolley hut.

As he approached, several of the crowd turned and started pointing at him. Most of them were laughing. He was horrified to see the full length figure of a man, naked from the waist down, his hand stuck up the jumper of a woman whose distinctive hairstyle and jewellery could not be mistaken. The man, whose perfectly knitted genitals were gently nudged by a forceful breeze, was unmistakably Gerald.

Too embarrassed to play a round now his womanising ways could no longer be shrugged off, he had no choice but to retreat and slink home — after having ripped down the offending wall hanging and shoving it into a wheelie bin.

Just One More Ball

By the time he arrived back home, Gerald was seething, his embarrassment turned to anger. But he was unable to take it out on an unsuspecting Cynthia, who was not alone. Sitting in his chair, quietly knitting a jumper for a small boy was the nuisance daughter of his latest conquest. The penny dropped.

"Hello dear," said Cynthia innocently. "Hope you don't mind, just having some knitters round for a get together. If you're quick, you can grab some of the shortbread in the kitchen. Put the kettle on while you're in there, thanks love."

"We're going to be meeting every Wednesday evening," Fay grinned at Gerald, "it's so kind of you and Cynthia to be so hospitable."

Cynthia carried on knitting. Gerald took up sailing.

Devon Time
Elizabeth Ducie

"Eurgh, what's that smell?"

"Smells like something's curled up and died. It's sort of dampish, animalish and dirty — yet somehow familiar." Ian, ten going on forty-seven and currently in a Sherlock Holmes phase, sucked on his imaginary Meerschaum pipe and tried to look knowledgeable.

"Cheese; maybe they've left some mouldy cheese behind?" I checked the fridge but it was empty.

"Damp! It's water! Oh god, I hope the stream hasn't flooded." Looking out of the window, I saw with relief the water level was low and the garden baked dry in the sunshine.

"Mum, it's stronger at this end of the hall."

As I followed Ian to the bottom of the stairs, I suddenly remembered our first visit to this cottage. We'd wandered around, accompanied by the proud owner — and an elderly, rotund golden retriever.

"Dog, it's wet dog! Ian, grab a pen and start a shopping list: air fresheners — lots of them. Come on Jenny; let's go find your room."

I took my three year old's hand and climbed the stairs.

The smell lingered for weeks, so strong I was half convinced they'd left the dog behind, or it had somehow found its way back again. I caught myself checking in cupboards and behind doors, just in case.

Surveying our new kingdom that Saturday afternoon, a silence fell on our little band, punctuated by an occasional addition to the shopping list.

"Pliers, we'll need pliers. All those nails — did they really have this many pictures?"

"Polyfilla for the holes."

"Cleaner for the bath — it's manky."

"I don't remember it being this shabby. Oh look, the carpet's all pulled up in here. Looks like the dog got shut in and tried to dig his way out."

"This ceiling's cracked — and there's a suspicious-looking stain. It's probably water, but could be blood." Sherlock was back.

Later that night, I got on the phone to my friend Mags. If I'd thought I'd get some sympathy, I was out of luck.

"You must be potty. Moving all that way. You'll know no-one. What happens if there's a problem, if one of the kids gets ill?"

"It'll be fine; I just felt —"

"I know you wanted to get away from London — stands to reason after what you've all been through. But really, I mean, Devon! It's like the other end of the world!"

"It's a beautiful cottage —"

"Come on, you'd only seen it once, must have been in it for an hour at most..."

"Twice actually, we went back the next day—"

"OK, twice — but it's not like you to act on a whim. Come on, you're the one who used to take all week and several trips around Bluewater to buy one pair of shoes. What's come over you?"

I tuned out her voice at that point. The cottage *was* perfect; within walking distance of shops and post-office but on the edge of the village, next to a stream. It was surrounded by farmland. The views of Dartmoor were superb. I'd been sure it was just what my family needed for a new start. Now I was beginning to wonder.

***

Two months later, I was even less sure I'd made the right decision. The cottage seemed to hate me. It was certainly doing its best to make me feel unwelcome. There'd been problems with the plumbing. Lights had fused at awkward moments, usually when it was pitch black outside — and none of the radiators seemed to work efficiently.

It wasn't just the cottage. I was beginning to think I wasn't cut out for village life at all. In London, I'd prided myself on my organisational skills. I'd always planned our menus a week ahead and done a 'big shop' with the family on Saturday afternoons. Sundays were spent cooking and freezing healthy nourishing meals for the coming week, in between washing and ironing Barry's shirts and my work clothes. I'd kept our little tribe together, even more so when Barry left us with no warning one dull November morning.

I'd been great at managing my time so I was able to get odd bits of shopping done and still have time for coffee with Mags during my lunch hour. Now, just popping to the shops for a couple of items seemed to take all morning.

It would start in the lane, where I always seemed to bump into someone eager for a chat. Often it was a very smartly dressed old lady, who took a daily walk along the lane, whatever the weather.

"Hello dearie, how are you settling in?"

"Er, hi Mrs —"

"Ellen — everyone calls me Ellen. Had enough of the 'Mrs' when I was at the school. Mind you, I enjoyed cooking for all the kids. I remember when…"

Twenty minutes later, we'd say our goodbyes and I'd be able to get on with my journey, looking at the scenery to remind myself why we were down here.

I learned that planning meals in advance was a waste of time. I'd get to the greengrocers, needing green and red peppers for chicken fajitas or aubergines for moussaka.

"Oh no m'dear, we don't have those very often — no call for them round here, see. How about some fresh spinach, picked from the garden this morning — or some nice caulis?'

Then there was the newsagents. Just popping in for a paper took almost an hour — on a good day. The queue usually stretched to the door and even with two people serving, it took ages to get to the front. Neil and Josie were a lovely couple, but they did like to gossip.

"Hello Annie, how's the old man, not seen him for ages. Yes, well, he's best to keep off it for a while in that case. Did you hear about Mrs Porter? She's got to go…" And so it would go on with each customer in turn.

One day, after a particularly wearying shopping trip, I decided to spend some time working on my special project.

"Come on Ian, I'm going to pull up that carpet in my bathroom. You can help me. There's another strange smell in there."

"But mum…"

"No arguments! Bring that Stanley knife with you. We can split the carpet up, it'll be easier to take to the dump that way."

"But mum..."

"NOW Ian. You can finish your book later."

With a resigned sigh, my son put down his tattered copy of *The Hound of the Baskervilles* and followed me upstairs.

One of the best assets of this property, as well as the surrounding countryside, fresh air, peace and quiet, was the master suite I'd taken for my own. There was a huge bedroom overlooking the fields, a walk-in wardrobe and a little bathroom. Much as I love my kids, there are occasions when I need to shut off and have some 'me time'. This was going to be my own little world. But first I needed to get it just right.

A few minutes later, we'd pulled up the carpet and were staring in horror at what lay beneath.

"Looks like the shower's been leaking at some point." Ian's good at stating the obvious. The floorboards were rotten and crumbled at a touch. I shuddered to think what might've happened if we'd left the carpet down much longer.

So that's how Old Jim the builder came into our lives. I was introduced to him a couple of days later. He was leaning on the garden fence, talking to a neighbour. A tall, wiry man, well into his seventies, his skin was the walnut brown of someone who spent most of their time outdoors. He came round, had a quick look at my bathroom and smiled reassuringly.

"No problem, me lover, I can sort this in a few days. I'll have that rotten board out in no time — but you're going to lose the shower cubicle."

"OK, we might as well get the whole thing done then. I was going to replace it at some point anyway." I looked at him, wondering how to put it tactfully. "That's not going to be too big a job for you, is it?"

"No, bless you, this is only a piddly little job, it'll take no time at all," he laughed. "Right, I'll come back tomorrow with some catalogues and you can pick out what you want. I've got a mate in the trade; he'll do us a good deal."

I heard nothing for a week then Old Jim knocked on the door one morning.

"Sorry I didn't get back before, bit of a problem on another job. Here's the catalogues I told you about. Just let me know what you want."

By the time I'd picked out the bath, the tiles and all the other bits and pieces, another week had gone by. Then we had to wait for everything to be delivered.

Four weeks after Old Jim had promised "a few days", he finally started work. First he took over the garage. In went his little work bench, his tile cutter, sheets of plasterboard and flooring. Then he took over the shelves in my dressing room with tools, buckets and bags of grout.

And so it began, the pattern of our days. He would arrive at nine — or ten — or one in the afternoon. He'd do a couple of hours work then disappear.

"Just got to go and get some more grout."

"I need a couple more tiles."

"Got to pick up my grandson Tommy from school, but I'll be back in the morning and we should have this finished by the end of the week — next Tuesday at the latest."

I'm not sure what was wrong. The old me would've sorted it out ages ago, but somehow, nothing I tried had any effect.

"Jim, I've got some friends coming to stay next month. I'm going to need this finished by —"

"Oh, that reminds me, dear, my son's coming home next week. I'll not be around for a couple of days, but it won't take long when I get back."

Two weeks later, I tried again.

"Jim, it would be great if we could clear —"

"Lovely time of year this — too nice to be indoors. Have you taken your kids letter boxing yet? No? Well, what are we waiting for? Give them a shout and I'll round up Tommy and get the car." So, instead of seeing more work done on the bathroom, I found myself in Jim's battered old Morris Minor with three excited kids in the back, heading for Dartmoor in search of hidden boxes.

Sometimes I was tempted to bring in someone else to sort it all out — but I didn't. He didn't seem to have much money, so I felt I couldn't take this job away from him. I was just glad I was paying him a fixed price, not by the day.

One winter's evening, we strolled into the village to watch the Christmas lights being switched on. Father Christmas led the parade of school-kids, including Ian. Jenny clung on to my hand, mouth open and eyes popping at the sight of Santa shaking hands and giving out sweets.

"Old Jim loves this time of year," said the woman standing next to me, "he's brilliant with the kids, isn't he?" I recognised her as one of the women who worked in the greengrocers.

"Old Jim?" I asked.

"In the Santa suit." She lowered her voice so Jenny couldn't hear her. "I hear he's doing some work for you," she went on. "You're so lucky."

I pulled a face, wondering whether lucky was the right word to use. Watching the parade, the woman carried on talking, not noticing my reservations.

"When he was younger, Jim did all the work in the village. Always made a lovely job of it — a real craftsman, he is. He's getting on a bit now, and he'll only take on jobs if he really likes someone. Yes, I reckon he must have taken a real shine to you and the kids."

So Old Jim was obviously a well-liked character in the village. I didn't want to risk upsetting my new neighbours, especially as the general opinion seemed to be he was doing me a favour.

The days stretched into weeks and the longer it went on, the harder it became to say anything. Christmas came and went. I was starting to think my special project would never be finished.

One morning at the start of the spring half-term week, I snapped, able to stand it no longer.

"Look, I don't care about the reasons. You promised me a few days would sort it — and that's six months ago. I want it done by the end of the week! This bloody house's getting on my nerves. I wish we'd never bought it."

Old Jim just smiled and nodded at me. "Relax me lover; there's plenty of time."

Exasperated, and just a little ashamed at my outburst, I stomped downstairs, leaving him to it. The phone was ringing. I grabbed the receiver and threw myself into an armchair, ready to rebuff the cold-calling salesmen who always seemed to ring around this time each day.

"Hello, this is Veronica Browne from Browne and Browne. Can I speak with Rosemary Ellis please?"

I sat bolt upright in the chair — Ronnie always had that effect on people.

"Ronnie, it's me — Rosemary," I said, trying to keep the surprise out of my voice. She was the last person I'd expected to hear from, especially after what we'd both said last time we'd been together.

"Rosemary, darling, I'm so glad I caught you in. How's life in the country? Ready to come back and do what you're best at, are you?"

"I thought you didn't need me. When you gave the job to Andy, you said —"

"Oh, Andy's moved on," she said airily and not at all abashed as she continued, "and you've always been the best office manager I've known. Come back — help me run the place — there'll be more money in it."

"Ronnie, can I ring you back — there's someone at the door," I fibbed.

As I disconnected the call, I could imagine her look of shock. No-one ever hung up on Veronica Browne, senior partner of one of the most exclusive literary agencies in the country. But I needed to think carefully before making a decision.

"Grandpa, come quick — it's happening." Suddenly, I heard shouting from outside. Tommy was standing in my front garden looking up at the bathroom window. Minutes later, Old Jim was in my kitchen.

"Come on then, grab your coat," he said, "you must see this. Ian, Jenny — you too."

Old Jim dragged me up the lane, with my kids trailing behind, Tommy dancing around in front urging us to hurry up. At the top of the lane, we crossed the stream and went into the farmyard. The kids ran on ahead. Old Jim and I followed more sedately.

As we entered the barn, I stopped suddenly — unsure whether to laugh or cry. My daughter was kneeling in a patch of mud gazing through a hole in the fence.

"Look Mummy, little lamb born."

Looking over the fence, I saw what had my daughter so entranced. In the corner lay one of the ewes, panting slightly and looking on as her offspring stumbled around on spindly legs. The little creature bleated feebly and nuzzled its mother, looking for food. Ian was sitting on top of the fence with Tommy, gazing open-mouthed.

Leaving the kids helping the farmer look after the new family, I strolled back down the hill with Old Jim. I found myself telling him about the call I'd just received.

"It will mean moving back to London, of course, and changing the kids' schools again. I'll keep this place as a holiday home — we'll need somewhere to retreat to every so often."

"Be a good job, will it?" Old Jim looked doubtful.

"It's what I've always wanted. I would be running the whole thing, organising the team, keeping the paperwork straight. I thought I'd get it when Mrs Ryland retired, but Ronnie brought in some young guy — said we needed a change of style. That didn't work out, so now I've got my chance." The last few words came out in a gulp and I realised there were tears rolling down my cheeks.

"I thought you were settling in really well here." Old Jim was staring across the fields towards Dartmoor, giving me time to rub my cheeks with the back of my hand.

"Oh, Jim, I don't know. The kids certainly love it, and it's much more peaceful than London, but I don't seem to fit in. I don't think I'm cut out for country living. Ronnie needs me. I don't seem to be much use to anyone down here."

"Hmmm." Old Jim gave me a long, considering look before heading for the stairs. "I'd better get on with this job then. You'll want it all sorted before you head back to London, won't you?"

I wandered back into the garden to gaze at orange and purple crocuses spread across the lawn. Daffodil buds were pushing through the soil and I found a tiny Primula in the sheltered flowerbed under the kitchen window. I'd been looking forward to seeing the garden develop over the months. Maybe I could get one of the neighbours to take a picture for me each week, so we'd have a full record of the time we missed.

"Hello Rosemary dear, do you have a few moments? I have something to ask you." Ellen, the retired school-cook, was standing at my gate.

"Come on in, Ellen. I was just going to put the kettle on. Stay and have tea."

As we sat in front of the fire, drinking tea and nibbling the ginger biscuits Ellen had baked that morning, she looked nervous, not her usual confident self. She pulled a large, dog-eared notebook out of her bag.

"I've wanted to ask you this for ages — but you've always seemed so busy. I've been doing some writing — just little tales about growing up around here, cooking for the kids, that sort of thing. It's all here, and I want something to give my grandchildren but I don't type, you see, and they're never going to be able to read my writing. Old Jim — you knew he was my brother-in-law, didn't you? — well, he suggested you might be able to help me put it into some sort of shape."

"Ellen, I'd love to help, but I'm not sure we'll be here…"

"Of course not — silly idea. Not to worry, dearie, I'm sure I'll find someone else to help me." She pushed the notebook back into the bag, a slight flush tingeing her carefully powdered cheeks. I leaned over and put my hand gently on her arm.

"Just let me think about it. I'm not sure what I'm going to be doing over the next few months, but I'll do what I can. More tea?"

After Ellen had left, I started getting some food ready for the kids, knowing they would come home as soon as their stomachs told them it was lunchtime.

Hearing the gate squeak, I pulled open the front door and called over my shoulder as I headed back to the kitchen.

"OK, you two — hands washed straight away, the soup's nearly ready."

"Well, that sounds wonderful, Rosemary, but are you sure you'll have enough for two extra?"

I spun around to see Neil and Josie from the newsagents standing on the door-step. I showed them in to the lounge, just as Ian and Jenny came running down the lane. I called up to Old Jim to tell him lunch was ready. Soon the six of us were tucking in to spiced carrot and apple soup with home-made bread.

"Well, this is a treat," Josie said. "We thought we'd pop in to see if you would be willing to join the volunteer driving rota. We take it in turns to run the older folk to church or the doctor."

"You've always seemed so busy before," Neil joined in, "but Jim rang me and suggested you might have some time on your hands. We'd be really glad of another volunteer."

I looked across the table, staring hard at Old Jim, but he was intent on finishing his soup and didn't seem to notice.

"Can I have a think about it?" I seemed to have been saying that a lot today.

After Neil and Josie had headed back up the lane towards the village and Old Jim had gone off to buy more grout, Ian and Jenny begged to go back to look at the lambs. Just before disappearing out of the door, Jenny ran and gave me a hug.

"What's that for?" I asked.

"She's really glad we live here," said Ian, "and I am too. We don't want to live anywhere else — ever."

Standing there I thought back to what had brought us here in the first place. We'd wanted to get away from the noise and rush of the city, wanted some peace and quiet. Even without the problems at work, I'd felt burnt out and in need of a change. Did I really want to go back to all that?

I reached for the phone and the local directory. First I phoned Ellen, then Neil and Josie. Finally, I dialled Ronnie's number. I didn't have to look that one up.

When Old Jim arrived back, he found me sitting by the fire, staring out of the window, just as the light was starting to fade.

"I reckon I'll have this done for you in another four days," he said.

"Sit down first and have a cup of tea, Jim," I said, "after all, there's plenty of time, isn't there?"

One Too Many
Sharon Cook

It was not love at first sight. Attraction — of course. An underlying antagonism — I'm sure. Admiration — a given. I could have chosen to walk away. Instead, I ruined three lives. I didn't care. Until I realised one of them was mine.

***

Two years later I found myself in the same bar. No longer wearing a wedding ring, I felt weary. She was there, as arranged. She looked stunning. With more time to work on her appearance than before, Lara seemed even more beautiful. More unattainable. She smiled. So did I.

"White wine spritzer, old girl?" she enquired, innocently.

"Please. It's hot outside. And seeing as I no longer drive…" The pain flickered across her face. It was momentary, intimate.

"We agreed," she said, "not to go there. It's over and done with."

"Then why did you come?" I asked, genuinely curious.

"I didn't want the last time we met to be in a court room."

"So this is the last time then? This is it. All over? Consigned to the past. The very last time. Ever?"

"We both know it's for the best." She was right. It was.

When Lara and I had met I was a high-powered businesswoman fresh out of a meeting, a City merger in the palm of my hand. By 9pm that evening I was elated at the outcome, relieved the previous six months had paid off and I needed to let off steam before returning home. My husband, a train ride away, was waiting to discuss future plans.

He'd be there, an Indian takeaway in the oven — on low — he knew my vagaries. The white wine would be in the fridge, three bottles of Sancerre. He wouldn't have started without me.

I'd downed three large vodka and Slimlines before I saw Lara. Gay bars are always dimly lit. We all look so much better that way. We chatted. She was a businesswoman too. Her clothes and make up were as expensive as her perfume — she was clearly an Alpha female, hence the antagonism. But we liked each other.

I had to get a taxi home, even though we'd only checked into the hotel for a couple of hours. My husband was fuming by the time I got in, soon after 3am. He had no idea where I had actually been. But he had wanted to talk. We did, eventually. He made his position very clear.

"Look, Erin," he said, "I want children, you know I do. I think I've waited long enough and time is ticking." I knew it was make or break for us. I also knew I loved my husband very much. If I was ever going to have a child, it would be with him or with no one. Alan understood so much of me and he had always supported me. People laughed when they discovered I was married to a baker. How could such a high flyer in the City actually be married to a baker? All the jokes about 'nice buns' eventually went away. We were content with each other. He baked cup cakes and foccacias for celebrities; I merged companies in hotels and bars across Europe.

What Alan didn't know was that I also did quite a bit of my own merging in hotel rooms across Europe. He never knew I liked women. It had simply never occurred to him. Why would it? We knew how to enjoy each other. Oh yes, we certainly knew how to love each other. That had been evident within hours of meeting. But how much of our hidden selves do we actually share with others? Even within the most intimate of set ups there are ravines never visited.

Alan went away on his annual fishing weekend with his 'lads'. So I took the car and drove Lara out into the Home Counties for a country weekend away. Lush hotel, great restaurants, gentle walks. A chance to, probably, say goodbye.

On the Saturday night, we drove to a Gastro pub all the Sunday supplements were raving about. Between us we drank far too much wine and, being out in the sticks, there were no taxis. I decided it would be fine to drive back to the hotel. Lara said she thought it was probably not a good idea, but she also said there was no way she was walking all that way in her Jimmy Choos. For two such clever women we were remarkably stupid that night.

By the time the police were called we had been trapped in the ditch for more three hours. Lara had to have her left leg amputated, above the knee.

I got prosecuted for driving whilst under the influence of alcohol. I had no defence. I think the judge probably took pity. I'll never have children now, the accident wrote off my pregnancy.

Had the judge known we were lesbians — and me married — I'm sure he would have taken a different view. No one actually knew, we were just off on a girlie weekend, weren't we?

Alan could not cope with my lack of support. He was devastated at the loss of our chance to become parents. I hadn't even known I was pregnant and took it all as a sign that I would have made a terrible mother.

I just couldn't be there for Alan. He was definitely the 'female' in our marriage. He divorced me on the grounds of 'unreasonable behaviour'. It was uncontested.

We talk occasionally. He met a lovely woman through an up-market, on-line dating site and they are already painting the nursery in our old house.

***

Lara brought me back into the moment.

"So how have you been — really?" she inquired, a gentleness evident in her voice.

"I can honestly say, I don't really know. Life is busy. I have a new home, on the wilds of Dartmoor. I couldn't carry on working in the City. Couldn't face it. I have a bicycle. I'm not 'the only gay in the village'" We both laughed at the comic reference.

"I'm not happy. I'm not unhappy. I'm in therapy." I looked directly at her. "Lara, can I ask you the same question?" She sipped her sparkling mineral water, her pale pink lipstick intact, before replying.

"My life is different too. I met a man — can you believe it, I met a man and it's good. We met at art school. He was my lecturer — there are so many advantages to being a mature student." As Lara laughed I felt a pang. It wasn't just her beauty that had drawn me to her, it was her lust for life — her lust for so much. Our connection had been casual, yet far deeper than I had ever realised.

"There's something else I want to tell you Erin," Lara took a deep breath, "I'm pregnant."

***

I don't know how I got through the rest of that lunchtime drink, the last thing I ever shared with Lara. On the train back to Devon, I managed to get a quiet corner seat in a first class carriage. It was only then I realised tears were streaming down my face. I couldn't stop.

When the doctors had told me I'd been carrying twins I think I just went numb. I destroyed three lives that day. I really hadn't cared. I hadn't cared until I realised one of them was mine.

The Stories of Pavel and Yuri
Elizabeth Ducie

"Uncle Sasha's going to fire me for sure." Gazing through the window at the plane on the runway, novice journalist Pavel sighed. Just then, two men left the terminal carrying a large sack between them. Pavel could have sworn he saw the sack move.

Grabbing his camera, he started taking pictures. The men were too far away to notice and he was completely engrossed in watching them. Suddenly he heard footsteps and, too late to do anything about it, he saw a reflection in the plate glass of a security officer who was standing right behind him. He was several centimetres taller than Pavel and the grey shirt of his uniform fitted tightly across his muscular chest.

"Stop! No pictures! Give that to me." The man snatched Pavel's camera. He pointed at a large notice just above their heads — a camera in a red circle with a black line across it. Pavel hadn't even noticed.

"Look I'm really sorry — I'll stop. I'll delete the pictures — but you can't take my camera. I need it for my job." Pavel knew he was babbling, but he couldn't afford to lose the camera as well as not having a story.

"Come to my office. We will discuss this further." The man turned and walked away, clearly expecting to be followed. Pavel shuffled after him.

The man closed the office door behind Pavel and pointed to a chair in front of the desk. He took an ornate key from his pocket and opened a massive safe in the corner of the room. Taking out a single sheet of paper, he relocked the safe before slotting the paper into an electric typewriter and adjusting the carriage. He looked up at Pavel.

"Now, tell me who you are and why you're taking pictures in my airport."

Pavel was still getting over the surprise of seeing a safe used as a stationery cabinet and an airport official using a typewriter, instead of a word processor. It was too much to take in on top of the shock of having his camera confiscated. Unthinking, he started speaking:

"I'm trying to save my job. My uncle sent me to find a story. I can't find anything to write about — and if I go back to Kiev without one, he'll fire me. I saw the two men carrying a sack — it moved. I thought it looked dodgy, so I took a few pictures…"

His voice faded as he realised he could be in real trouble here. If the men were up to no good, they were doing it openly — which meant this security man probably knew what was going on.

The man stared at him for a long moment. Pavel shrank back in his seat, holding his breath.

"Keep talking."

"I work for Sasha Petrovich, editor of *Kiev Today*. He's married to my mother's sister — I think that's the only reason I've still got a job. Someone mentioned the result of your mayoral election is in dispute — so I came to see if I could find a story."

"You're no good as a writer?"

"Actually, I'm a pretty good writer," snapped Pavel. "I'm writing a novel in my spare time — and I've had quite a few short stories published already. It's the reporting I can't do," he admitted meekly. "Talking to strangers is so difficult and no-one wants to tell me anything."

"So, you thought you'd find something scandalous to write about our new mayor? Did you uncover anything?"

Pavel shook his head, wondering how much he should say. He still didn't know how much trouble he was in. A couple of days ago, he'd heard a rumour that black marketeers from Moscow had financed the winner's campaign. An old friend had set up a meeting for him with "someone on the inside." They'd met in a broken down coffee shop on the edge of town.

"Yes, I can tell you all about it," the spotty youth had said, "but it's going to cost you." Pavel only had 100 grivna on him; barely enough to buy dinner in one of the newer restaurants in the centre of town, but the youth had snatched the banknote from him and stuffed it in his pocket without a second glance.

"The Mayor's got a cousin who works in Moscow — on a construction site. And he's married to a Russian who's been here in L'viv helping with the election campaign..." Sensing there was no real story, Pavel had tuned out at this point and stared through the window onto the darkening streets. When he started listening again, his companion was talking about a scam featuring old ladies collecting kopeks outside the cathedral.

Now, Pavel realised with a start, the security man was drumming his fingers on the desk and looking at him over the top of his glasses.

"It looks like the rumours are unfounded. I had a quick interview with the Mayor himself, but nothing came out of it — he's a very busy man, of course."

***

What he didn't say was that more could probably have come of the interview if he'd managed to get any sensible questions asked. After four days of following leads that went nowhere, he'd run out of money and, terrified of returning to Kiev without a story, made one final attempt to get an interview with the Mayor. He'd failed to get through on each of the five previous occasions he'd tried to call. This time, he'd been successful. The Mayor had agreed to see him for a few minutes that morning. There was just time before Pavel had to leave for the airport.

He had hurried over to the Town Hall and was quickly ushered in to the Mayor's office. He'd prepared all his questions and felt sure he was going to get an interview that would impress Uncle Sasha. As he'd sat waiting for the Mayor to finish a phone call, he'd glanced around the huge room — and had frozen, fighting for breath. One whole wall of the office was given over to glass cases — and there was movement in each one. Not the rapid movement that comes from mice, hamsters or birds — but the slow sinuous movement that comes from snakes, snakes of all colours and sizes. At that point, the Mayor had finished his call and looked at his watch.

"OK, young man, you've got eight minutes — what do you want to know?" Pavel had been so frightened of the snakes, all his questions had gone out of his head. The interview had not gone well and now he was about to fly home with no story for Uncle Sasha. And it looked like he'd lost his camera as well.

***

"OK, relax my friend." The security officer suddenly grinned across the desk at him and jumped to his feet. "I'll help you if you help me. Come, drink with me and we'll talk about it." When the words came, Pavel was not really surprised. He was reaching for his wallet when he heard the man laugh.

"I don't want your money. I want your words. You're a writer, aren't you?" Pavel was now really confused. The man continued.

"Look, I'm Yuri Mikailovich. I've been stuck in this office in this tin-pot airport for seventeen years. Everyone knows me — and everyone laughs at me. 'See,' I hear them say, 'Yuri has never caught anyone, never solved a crime, will never get the promotion he wants' — but how can I, when there are no crimes to solve? You understand my problem?"

Pavel nodded — although he wasn't sure he understood at all.

"Next week, we have a visit — the boss is coming from Kiev. He wants my report for the past year. As usual, I have nothing for him. And as usual, he will leave me here to rot."

"But I don't see — oh, the two men — you think they're criminals?" Pavel thought he understood. "You want my pictures as evidence?"

"Who, those two? No! They're just loading the plane — I'm talking about you!"

"Me?"

"Yes, you. You must help me write a report about a dangerous spy who came to L'viv to assassinate the boss. How he took pictures in the airport, planning the deed, how I caught him and how he refused to talk. How I interrogated him and how he finally cracked under pressure and confessed."

Pavel thought he saw a flaw in the plan.

"Won't he wonder why I'm not being held prisoner? Er — you're not going to hold me prisoner, are you?"

"Of course not. He's only here for a couple of hours. I'll tell him you've been sent back to Kiev."

"Well, OK, I'll do it," said Pavel, "but you're going to need more than one sheet of paper."

One hour, several sheets of paper and a bottle of vodka later, Pavel stood at the office door, camera in hand. Yuri's story was written and the report was ready for the boss's visit. Pavel's own story was buzzing around in his head — about the intrepid reporter who'd faced danger to get his story. How he'd been mistaken for a terrorist, arrested and interrogated. They'd even taken a picture of him, handcuffed to a chair. Uncle Sasha loved a good picture with his stories. Pavel turned to Yuri who was gazing out of the window across his little domain.

"Just one thing, Yuri," he said, "what was in that sack?" He saw his new friend's grinning reflection in the glass.

"Oh that's just Ivan the Terrible — one of the Mayor's pet snakes. It's grown so big, he's donated it to Kiev Zoo. Have a good flight back, my friend."

Tale of Two Gardens
Sharon Cook

As the flyers went up there was a flurry of interest. It was a first and the organisers were as anxious as the potential punters were intrigued. But there was no going back now. Those who had signed up would lose face if they backed out. And, quite frankly, those who had been too nervous to get involved had missed the boat.

It was hoped the East Spitwytch Open Gardens would become a regular feature on the mid-summer calendar of the Devon village which was, indeed, picture postcard. The village shop and Post Office testified to it. The Parish council had, however, shunned 'chocolate box', opting instead for their cherished village to adorn a range of up-market, clotted cream biscuits instead.

So much was riding on this first year. The Parish councillors hoped it would raise the profile of their tucked-away settlement and, in such cash-conscious times, every little shop owner hoped it would bring a few more customers their way.

Jack and Jill Wells — who had spent all their married life rebutting every joke possible — were delighted their shortlist contained 14 gardens.

"And they're all quite different," they told everyone. "You might already know some of them. But we've persuaded Lord and Lady Fosset at The Manor to open up their gardens, we have several in the village, one of the tithe cottages — yes, that's right, Olivia's place — and a glorious, really unusual garden on the banks of a lake, belongs to, erm, yes, that botany lecturer at Exeter University, that's right," enthused Jill Wells.

Oh yes, there was quite a buzz. Some of the locals were more than a little interested in the business of others, so the chance to go looking around new territory was just too tempting. And it was all for charity, raising cash for a children's cancer support group.

In the weeks leading up to the much anticipated event, each of the green-fingered volunteers — or their paid employees in the case of the Fossets — worked hard and prayed for the right weather. Old Stan was desperate for enough sun to bring on his fuchsias while young Bill wanted plenty of rays so he could show off a very impressive display of tomatoes.

The Hopkins at number 28 gave full vent to their OCD with a meticulously executed yet surprisingly stunning collection of conifers and grasses, while Mr and Mrs Boniface were both obsessed with anything that would grow in a pot, edible or otherwise. They hadn't been away on holiday for more than twenty years so they could tend all their 'beautiful babies', as Mrs B called them. Their garden was stunning; some compared it to the hanging gardens of Babylon with every nook and cranny devoted to plants. "Even aubergines," raved Jack.

One local worthy was showcasing a noted collection of twentieth century sculptures, against a background of immaculate lawns and well swept patios. There were a couple of real 'cottage gardens' and, of course, Olivia's garden.

Having 'blown in' to the village about ten years previously she had been eligible for one of the town's tithe cottages, in part as she was single mum to a disabled child. Her son, Robert, had cystic fibrosis and was frequently confined to a wheelchair. The two-bedroom cottage had been a Godsend to them both. Caring for her son, whose medical needs were constant, took most of Olivia's time. The garden was her sanity. When they arrived it had been little more than a tangle of weeds, an unloved patch of shrubs bordered by three ancient apple trees, a quince tree and, to Olivia's delight, a medlar tree.

As she peeled back the layers over the years, a beautiful herb garden emerged. She had replaced all the wooded-out rosemary and sage, grew lavender bushes from seed and re-planted every herb a half decent cook could ever wish for. And all to the original design. Much of the garden featured heavenly-scented roses to compliment all the other fragrant-rich plants, including several pale pink summer jasmines she had rescued from the chaos. They roamed freely among the shrubs lining the back fence, untethered in their beauty.

Olivia even created a small vegetable patch, which Robert adored. Against all the odds her glorious son had passed his thirtieth birthday and, though they had really bad days when she felt even the cottage hospital could never save him, Robert pulled through.

Olivia thanked the garden each time. And each time she said a silent prayer, she added a quirky offering. A giant tea cup filled with sedum spilling over the edge. An old, galvanised watering can planted up with bright red geraniums. An vintage enamel bread bin filled with peppery basil. A rusted pot bracket filled with a tiny tub of miniature ferns and nailed to the washing line post. Safe to say, it was a very quirky garden.

Having left home in her late teens, because of her illicit pregnancy, Olivia had faced many struggles. Eking out a meagre income on a series of market stalls selling bric-a-brac, the occasional good find had allowed her and Robert to survive.

Some deeply hidden instinct had drawn her back to East Spitwytch just as the tithe cottage had become vacant. The terrace of five cottages was administered by a trust, originally set up by a benevolent member of the Fosset family, who had lived at The Manor since the seventeenth century. The inalienable right of 'parish paupers' was set in stone, and allowed anyone who met a list of strict criteria to apply for residence at a subsidised rent. Olivia applied, and the board of trustees agreed she must be allowed to reside at the cottage for as long as she was able to pay the rent.

Opening up the garden felt like an honour to Olivia, her way of saying thank you to the village. She was intrigued to see that The Manor was also opening up. Olivia sighed. Despite the hardships, she was content. Soon to turn fifty she looked more like forty. Laughing quietly to herself as she looked in a pretty Venetian mirror hanging in her hallway, Olivia reckoned struggle proved to be a better face cream than anything money could buy. There was just time to prune the Iceberg rose, it was going to be spectacular in its icy whiteness by Saturday.

***

Up at The Manor, Howard Fosset was remarkably unhappy. The fifty-eight year old Lord was beginning to feel his age, not helped by the fact he'd been stupid enough to take a third wife after the first two had failed to produce any children. His current Croatian spouse had just turned twenty-six and, having delivered a daughter, was refusing to even think about trying for a son and heir. In fact Lord Fosset had been barred from his pretty young wife's bedroom since the birth of his only child.

Friends had warned him that Adrianne was probably after nothing more than a title, large house and generous allowance. But what Howard Fosset wanted, he got. Some said he got what he deserved. A loveless marriage and a philandering wife who ran up huge bills in London hotels. It was the same deal his first wife had endured at his hands.

The day before the open garden event he was particularly unhappy. The garden was looking glorious, thanks to a team of skilled and dedicated gardeners. But his floozy of a wife had decided they would offer cream teas; such charity gestures always helped to make her feel somewhat superior. Any opportunity to show off, to 'Lady' it over the villagers. Lord Fosset hated giving money away. He'd close down the Tithe cottages if he could, sell them on as second homes to rich bankers. Much better than keeping that damn trust going. Still, at least he'd have some peace over the weekend. With his wife doing her 'Lady Bountiful' act he could slope off and watch the racing on telly, without being expected to do anything domestic.

***

Saturday dawned bright and clear, a small miracle in such a wet summer. Garden gates opened and people 'oohed' and 'ahhhed' their way around the gardens. Olivia was very touched by the comments she received, and even agreed to go and give the local WI a talk about how she had rediscovered the garden.

"It's not quite Heligan," she remarked, "but we do have some striking plants."

That evening Howard Fosset was forced to listen to his wife's ramblings about the day.

"And you must to go visit the garden at the poor cottages," she droned on in her thick accent, which had once entranced but now appalled him. "Is beautiful. Lovely lady. Her boy in a chair with wheels. She have many herbals and a beautiful ice rose. Um no, not of ice made but of white. She told me rose called 'Iceberg'. It same rose as in our rose garden I think, no?"

Despite his irritation, Howard was listening. His great grandmother had planted the rose garden with the Icebergs after his great grandfather was lost to The Titanic. But then again, it was not an uncommon rose.

"And we raise more than £700 pounds for the sick children families," beamed Lady Fosset.

"Blimey," thought Lord Fosset, maybe tea rooms aren't such a bad idea. He should mention it to his management team again.

By the Sunday morning Lord Fosset's curiosity had got the better of him. There was no danger of his being recognised by the *hoi polloi*, he thought smugly, as he refused to mix with them.

Setting off as his wife put up tables on a back lawn — overlooking the magnificence of the Victorian glasshouses — Lord Fosset revved up the Range Rover and set off, with just one garden in mind. Parking up by a bank outside the Tithe Cottages, he soon found the 'open garden' sign. Wandering around the side of an end terrace he was surprised to find himself in quite a large garden. Wondering if the poor should really be allowed such large gardens distracted him momentarily.

It was impossible not to be drawn in by the beauty of the place. Yet it wasn't just the plants, the blooming flowers, an immaculate vegetable garden, and climbers trailing up stakes and between tripods made of stripped branches. It wasn't the heavenly smell emanating from so many different directions. The garden had a serenity which slowed his footsteps, urging him to explore every inch of its divine loveliness.

As he wandered around he kept seeing oddities: purple pansies poking out of the top of a child's green wellington; a small sundial balanced on a mottled grey stone, delicate ivy tendrils seeming to glue the two together; tiny alpine plants patchworking their way around the edge of a border planted with majestic lilies.

And then he saw the rose, the Iceberg in its splendid whiteness tinged with a hint of pink in the very centre, so subtle it could hardly be seen. How had he never appreciated the magnificence of all those planted in his very own gardens?

"Hello Howard," said an oddly familiar voice. Turning, Howard tried to retain a modicum of composure as he faced the sister he had not seen for more than 30 years.

"Hello Olivia," he said, attempting an expression of benevolence but which looked more like a grimace. "Lovely garden," he managed to stutter. "It must take someone a lot of time looking after this little lot."

"Yes Howard, it does take up much of my time," smiled Olivia.

"You! It's your garden?" bellowed Howard, "how on earth...?"

"Even someone born with a silver spoon in their mouth," remarked Olivia, "can fall on hard times."

"But, but..." huffed Howard.

"Save it, dear brother," laughed Olivia. "Oh, and I gather my son Robert has a cousin. Bluebell Snowflake, she's two isn't she? I'd love them to meet some time. And your daughter, not even begat by the unfortunate Agatha who, I believe, eventually saw sense and ditched you. And then, what was her name? Tanya wasn't it? Fabulous horsewoman," grinned Olivia, now in such full flow Lord Fosset was unable to stop her. "So how's it going with wife number three?"

Several other garden visitors had become aware of the exchange and, mindful of her own position rather than that of her pompous brother, Olivia invited him in to her kitchen for a cup of tea.

"Bet it's the first time you've ever set foot in one of these charming cottages," she goaded, gently. Howard was quite stunned, and followed, silently, his mind a jumble of unspoken thoughts. He'd have whipped out his hip flask to top up the tea had he felt able to share with this woman. Instead he glowered, like a small child caught smashing a window.

"I do know, Howard, how painful it must have been for you and Agatha, unable to have a child. Me getting caught out like that. I was only 19, it was... unfortunate. But it was no reason to banish me. You do know Agatha never even wanted children, don't you? It was expected of her though, wasn't it?"

Howard could think of nothing he wanted to say — out loud.

"You told mummy and daddy all sorts of things about me that weren't true. I know you did. But you know what Howard, it doesn't matter. My life has taken its own course and, well, Robert is—" At that moment a tall, good looking young man strolled into the kitchen, cradling several bunches of fresh cut flowers.

"Oh, sorry mum. Didn't realise you were busy, just need those secateurs," he said, wheezing quite heavily.

"That's OK love," said Olivia. "Meet your Uncle Howard."

Robert smiled, stretched out his hand and shook the one limply proffered. "Pleased to meet you sir. I hope you enjoy the garden. Must be off, customers waiting," he grinned and strode out of the small kitchen.

"I didn't even know you were here," mumbled Howard.

"Well why would you? I was told quite plainly I wasn't welcome, and what would happen if I returned. I hear the garden still looks beautiful, especially the roses," added Olivia, steering the conversation back to the present.

Distractedly Howard mumbled "yes", trying to remember something deeply buried.

"Do you still see erm, his dad, Robert's dad? asked Howard, who had never known who fathered his only nephew.

"Yes, actually. We're great friends — he helped me write the gardening book. You must buy a copy, all the proceeds are going to charity. Cystic Fibrosis as it happens."

"He helped you write a gardening book?" realisation dawning on Howard.

"Yes Howard. A gardening book. Well, it was hardly going to be *Lady Chatterley's Lover*, was it?" laughed Olivia, realising only then that her brother never knew Robert's dad had risen to become head gardener at The Manor. It was how she acquired the Iceberg rose, which she felt gave her a direct link to her own heritage, despite the family ties so cruelly pruned by a bitter brother and parents bound by outdated conventions.

"Look Howard, I'd better get back to the garden. It's quite busy out there and I don't want Robert on oxygen by this afternoon." Only then did Howard notice the pipes running around the wall into the living room, an oxygen canister leaning against the side of the fridge. "Here," added Olivia with a flourish. "I'll sign a book for you. The donation bucket is on the way out."

***

Later that evening Howard was sat in his leather armchair in the back conservatory, overlooking the manicured lawns contained within rigid lines of box hedging, all leading down to a large, very formal lake, not a folly in sight. A whisky bottle sat on the Indian wicker table; a bottle opened just a few hours earlier. It was only half full, though his glass was virtually empty.

He stared again at the dedication inside Olivia's book, tears streaming down his ruddy cheeks: *To my son who has shown me humility through his disability. And to my brother, who ensured my life was my own.*

Business as Usual
Elizabeth Ducie

It started with a news flash on Radio 4.

"It's eleven o'clock on Tuesday 18th March and here are the headlines. Consumer goods giant Stratters has launched a takeover bid for rival company, Bingley. Estimated to be worth nearly 10 billion pounds, the deal is the latest in a series —"

The newsreader's voice was lost in static as the car entered the Blackwall Tunnel. By the time it emerged a few minutes later, the news bulletin was over and Joanne Walker's car-phone was ringing.

"Jo, this is Henry — where are you?"

"About thirty minutes away. The meeting finished early."

"Good. I wanted to check you'd be here — departmental meeting at noon."

"Henry, I've just heard the news. Looks like the rumours were true after all?"

"Yes — looks like it. See you later, then. Bye..." Her boss broke the connection and was gone.

Joanne was always happy to stand in for Henry at the monthly briefing meetings. It was not far from her one-bedroom flat in Blackheath to the red and white striped brick Bingley House on Old Kent Road. This was the building where it all began. Before growing demand for their products had pushed manufacturing to other countries with cheaper workforces. Even before health regulations had forced the purchase of a purpose-built factory outside London. In those early days, batches of skin cream and vats of toothpaste had been mixed in the basement and hauled up to the third floor for filling into pots and tubes. The company's tiny museum displayed pictures of smiling operators in white coats and frilly hats standing next to packing tables, while in the background, lace curtains waved gently in the breeze from open windows.

The engineer in Joanne fully understood why today's Packing Hall, housing noisy automatic filling machines, was clad in stainless steel with controlled environments and windows that were never opened. This didn't stop the romantic in her spending the drive from HQ to the factory dreaming of being part of those tranquil scenes from the past. Except today. Today she finished the journey in a daze. The suburbs gave way to Kent countryside and the sun glistened unnoticed on the water as she crossed the Medway. Even the new-car smell of her hard-won company BMW failed to penetrate her senses.

By the time Joanne reached the meeting room, it was just a few minutes before noon. Listening to the hubbub of comments, the level of anxiety was obvious to her.

"Of course, there's going to be job losses..." Annie the cleaner was saying to her mate Phyllis. The two had worked in the department for nearly twenty years, knew everyone's birthday and wedding anniversary off by heart and could always be relied upon to have the kettle boiled when a cup of tea was needed.

"They're much bigger than us..." project manager Bob was confiding to his secretary Alice. They were never far apart during working hours — or at other times, if the rumours were true.

"There goes the Japanese expansion project..." said Stan the design engineer who had spent the best part of six months preparing plans and budgets and was due to present his proposal to the Board next month.

Joanne had worked for Henry in International Operations for three years and had been his deputy for just six months. This team of engineers, project managers, secretaries and domestic staff was family. A huge, chaotic, sometimes fractious, family of thirty-seven. Her fears for them were greater than her own concerns. She was young, single and confident of getting another job 'if the worst happened'. It wouldn't be so easy for some of the others.

Everyone fell silent as Henry Miles arrived and strode to the front of the room. He was wearing his trade-mark charcoal suit and striped shirt with white collar, but his thick grey curls stood to attention where anxious fingers had been pulling at them.

"OK, I'm sure you've all heard the news," Henry said. He sat back casually against the corner of the table as Joanne had often seen him do before, but this time, instead of stuffing his hands in his pockets, he had his arms crossed tightly over his chest. "Stratters has put in a bid. But that's all it is for now — a bid. We don't know what's going to happen. The Board's going to meet later this week to make its decision."

"Come on, Henry, you must know more than that — are our jobs at risk?" The question came from one of the engineers sitting in the corner, but from the nods around the room, he was voicing everyone's fears.

"Look, I'm sorry — I don't know any more than you guys. For now, all we can do is get back to our desks and keep going. Remember folks, business as usual. Jo, can you pop in and see me after lunch?"

With that, Henry headed back to his office and, for once, closed the door. The others started drifting off to their desks. But the buzz of speculation continued.

When Joanne poked her head around the door of Henry's office a couple of hours later, he was standing at the window, looking over the factory buildings to the farmland and woods beyond.

"I'd miss this view, Jo," he said. "When I was first interviewed for this department, old Bill Nichols asked me where I wanted to be in ten years — and I said 'here in your office, Bill'. It actually took me closer on fifteen— but I got it in the end."

As he talked, Henry picked up the binoculars, which always sat ready on the windowsill, and followed the passage of a seagull as it took off from the roof of the Packing Hall and gradually dwindled in the distance, heading towards the sea.

"Forty-eight I've spotted, you know. Forty-eight different species of birds since I've been in this office. I was hoping to pass the fifty mark, but I'm not sure that's going to happen now."

"Henry, is there something you're not telling us?" Joanne had never seen her boss like this. He was normally so positive about everything. In fact, the one criticism she'd sometimes heard levelled at this popular manager was 'Henry Miles is such a yes-man, he'll never question anything pronounced from on high.'

But, as quickly as it had started, the moment was gone. Henry put down the binoculars, ran his fingers through his curls and gestured Joanne to a seat.

"No, nothing like that," he said. "I just think we need to keep an eye on the troops over the next few days. This whole thing might have gone away by this time next week and I don't want us to lose a week's work on pointless speculation. Between the two of us, I want to cover as many of the project meetings as possible. Just to make sure they keep on track."

"Makes sense," Joanne said, reaching for her diary, "which ones do you want me to do?"

***

Three days later, on Friday 21st March, Henry called another meeting. Same meeting room. Same group of people. But this time he didn't sit on the table. He stood with his back pressed against the smooth white wall they normally used as a presentation screen. Before he said anything, he took off his John Lennon-style glasses and gave them a good polish. He cleared his throat and pushed the glasses back on his nose.

"An announcement has just gone out from Stratters headquarters." He kept glancing at the paper in his hand, as though checking the words were still the same. "Their offer's been accepted. The merger will go through in the next few weeks."

Questions came from all over the room. Henry held up his hands, 'like a teacher,' thought Joanne, 'stemming the play-time rush.'

"All we know for now is the deal will go through. For the moment, it's just business as usual."

Joanne used the same phrase on the phone to Ray Brookes in California later that day. The pair had been good friends since her first visit to the US plant just over a year before. He'd taken her to a baseball game in his

1950s Oldsmobile. She'd completely failed to understand the rules, but had loved the atmosphere and grazed all afternoon on hot-dogs and giant pretzels. Now she was trying to set up a teleconference for the US project they were both working on — but Ray was proving difficult to pin down.

"Business as usual — what are you talking about? Geez you Brits are unbelievable," he barked. "Don't you realise this business will never be the same again?" It was a conversation Joanne was to think back on many times in the next few weeks.

***

The merger, as the Stratters board insisted on calling it, was finalised on Thursday 1st May and Bingley became part of Stratters-Bingley. A brand new logo appeared everywhere. Overnight, company signs, letter headings and advertising material took on the new name — and just like that, the Bingley Bunny was gone. Ever since George Bingley, the company's founder, started selling tooth-cleaning powders from a bicycle in the 1880s, the little rabbit had been there. Every piece of paper, every cardboard box, every company vehicle carried its image. Mothers in rural villages in Africa or in the Amazonian rain-forest, unable to read, placed their trust in the packs of soaps and washing powder carrying the picture of the 'long-eared one'. Now it was no more.

For Joanne and her colleagues in International Operations, the implications of the new organisation started to become apparent the very next day.

"Jo, this is Mike Evans from Kenya," said a voice on the phone that afternoon. "I've got two blokes from Stratters here. They're telling me I now report to the MD of the Stratters factory on the other side of town. And I can't sign a cheque for more than £20 without authority. That can't be right, can it?"

"Mike, I've no idea — let me check and get back to you," Joanne said. She dropped the phone and raced along the corridor to Henry's office. He was sitting at his desk and stared silently at her as she recounted her call from Kenya.

"I don't understand," she finished. "Mike's doing a great job over there. Why should he be treated like this?"

"Jo, it's not just Mike," Henry said. "In the past hour I've heard that Miguel in Mexico has just been fired, the German factory's been switched to part-time working, and I've just received the new organisational structure for the US plant." He pushed a strip of fax paper across the desk towards her.

"But these are some of our best General Managers. Why would we want to get rid of them?"

Henry gave a sigh and shook his head.

"The thing is, Jo, all the countries where we have plants have a least one Stratters factory as well. We won't need more than one General Manager — in fact, we probably won't need more than one factory in most places."

"But these are good people — our friends as well as our colleagues. Isn't there anything you can do to steer the decisions —"

"Jo, I don't have any say in all this." Henry's smile looked forced to Joanne, and it certainly didn't reach his eyes. "The Board's deciding who gets the jobs and I'm only being told of the changes as they occur. But the Board will know what they're doing."

As she left the office, Joanne reflected on Henry's phrase 'we won't need...' She also realised the 'business as usual' mantra was gone from his conversation. She started keeping a record of the appointments as they were made. Within a week, fifty General Managers had been appointed world-wide. All but one were former Stratters employees.

***

On Friday 9th May, everyone in the company was invited to a briefing meeting with the Chairman and other members of the Stratters-Bingley Board. The announcement promised a question and answer session. The only room large enough to accommodate everyone was the ballroom in the club-house. With its dusty, faded red velvet curtains, 1970s-style patterned carpet and disco glitter ball, it had seen many a Christmas party, retirement do or wedding reception. Joanne had been there just a couple of weeks before, when one of the engineers had married a girl from the Packing Hall. Between them, the couple could name twelve relatives from three generations who used to work for Bingley. It was that sort of company. Every party turned into a reunion at some point.

In the daylight, Joanne thought the ballroom looked shabby and unfriendly. It was packed with more than a thousand employees, and she found the body language telling. The bright young management trainees were all sitting at the front, eager to hear how their futures would be enhanced by the new regime. The engineers sat in groups around the room, wearing sceptical, seen-it-all-before expressions. Joanne was most struck by the attitude of the machine operators. Slumped in their chairs, some whispered nervously while others stared silently at the floor.

Chairman of the Board, Sir Reginald Soames, sat on the stage, flanked by three other former Stratters Directors and the ex-Bingley Personnel Director who had been given responsibility for 'Special Projects' within the new organisation. Soames was familiar to everyone. He'd been on television quite a bit, especially in the past month. His navy, pin-striped suit was uncrumpled and his tasselled, black leather loafers reflected the spotlight directed on him from above. His companions chatted quietly together, but he silently watched as the people took their seats. When he rose to speak, he used no notes. His speech was eloquent, conciliatory and just a little too smooth for Joanne's liking.

"We're making history here," Soames said, with a sweeping gesture to the furthest corners of the room. "I'm proud to be part of this exciting project — and you should be, too. Times are changing and we need to change with them. We're merging two of the oldest, and most successful, companies in this industry to make a new organisation, fit for purpose."

But, it was his closing comments that left Joanne open-mouthed with disbelief.

"I know some of you are worried about your jobs. I understand, believe me, I do. It's going to take a while for us to get the details sorted, but you can be assured we are taking the best from both companies to put together a great team for the future."

"Well, if you really are taking the best from both organisations," Joanne wanted to shout out, "can you tell us why you've just spent 9.6 billion on such a crap company?"

Throughout the question and answer session, Joanne thought of that forty-nine to one appointment score and wished she had the nerve to ask her question. But she didn't. Nobody asked it. The meeting finished soon after and everyone filed out of the ballroom in silence. There wasn't anything else to say.

***

Throughout the rest of the year, the obliteration of Bingley continued. Some people fought to keep their old identity alive.

"Hey Joanne," Stan the design engineer said, when she bumped into him at the new beverage machine one morning in July, "I think I've worked out the difference between people from Bingley and people from Stratters."

"Not sure there's supposed to be a difference, is there Stan?" she replied.

"Well, we've accepted we work for Stratters-Bingley. But they still think they work for Stratters."

Stan stirred his tea, blew on it, took sip and pulled a face.

"Yuk — come back Annie, all is forgiven. Oh, by the way," he continued, "the Japanese proposal's going to the Board next month. Pity they had to check all my calculations before they accepted them — but hey, that's the Stratters way!"

When Joanne returned to her office, the latest copy of *Stratton Trek* was lying on her desk. The authors of the underground press were never discovered, but for a brief few weeks that summer, former Bingley employees thrilled to the exploits of 'Strattons on the starboard bow', attempting to invade a spaceship but continually repelled by the plucky little Bingloids.

Henry was never heard to use the phrase 'business as usual' again. He was seconded to the Integration Task Team and spent eighteen months helping close down the factories he'd worked so hard to set up over the previous twenty-two years. His plans to hold a Bingley Bunny memorial party on the first anniversary of the merger were abandoned when his Director — a bright young thing from the Stratters management training scheme — told him 'it would be inappropriate'. Henry took early retirement at the end of November and set up a successful consultancy practice, advising companies in the developing world on factory refurbishments. Two months earlier, he'd spotted his fiftieth species when a Lesser Whitethroat rested in the tree outside the office on its migration flight south.

Joanne took over Henry's office briefly, before they were all moved to a brand new section of the Stratters-Bingley headquarters, built on the site of the main Stratters UK factory in Staffordshire. She still had her apartment in Blackheath which she used sometimes at the weekends, but bought a tiny cottage in a small village six miles from the new site.

***

Five years later, Joanne was working through her emails one Monday morning when her phone rang.

"Jo, this is Henry. Are you online?" It was a while since they'd spoken.

"Henry, how are you?"

"Go to the BBC website, Jo. You'll want to see this. The bastards are at it again. I'll call you later." Joanne stared at her phone. Her former boss's phone manner hadn't improved since he'd left. Then she turned back to her computer. The BBC website was the usual hodgepodge of politics, royal stories and sport. Joanne almost missed the single line of text running across the top of the screen:

"Breaking News: Overwoods and Stratters-Bingley in merger talks."

Rumours were flying round the company by the time Joanne got an email from the Board two hours later. She called to her secretary through the open office door.

"Marion, can you round up the team? Tell them I'm holding a meeting in thirty minutes." She made a few calls to colleagues within the company, all of whom were as surprised by the news as she was. Then she headed for the meeting room. She could hear the voices before she was through the door.

"Do you think there'll be redundancies?" Shirley Evans sounded tearful. She had only just been recruited as a secretary, after two years on the dole.

"They've got a lot more factories than us," said Norman Ford, who had recently returned to his engineering post after paternity leave following the birth of his third child.

As Joanne walked to the front of the room, the hubbub of chatter died down. She gazed at the group she'd assembled over the past few years. There were a couple of members of Henry's old team, sitting at the back, looking relatively sanguine. She knew at least one of them was already looking for redundancy.

The rest of her team had all come from the Stratters side of the company. Even now, five years down the line, it was difficult not to think in terms of Strattons and Bingloids. They were looking at her with a mixture of fear and confusion on their faces.

'Welcome to my world,' she thought as she glanced at the print-out in her hand and cleared her throat.

"OK, everyone, I'll keep this short. You've all heard the news reports. The Board is in discussion with Overwoods. It's unlikely any decision will be made before this time next week."

A ripple of sound ran around the room and a couple of people opened their mouths to ask questions, but Joanne held up her hands to forestall them.

"I'm sorry, folks — that's really all I know for now. We've just got to carry as normal for the time being. Remember — business as usual."

The Outcasts
Sharon Cook

Each morning, on the way back from the school, Thea's heart sank. She was delighted at being able to walk Immy to school, loved seeing her skip off, pausing to turn and wave with her usual: "Bye bye, love you!" Watching the smiling six-year old never failed to bring a lump to her throat. Thea had learnt to fight back the tears.

In fact Thea smiled at anyone and everyone as if it were truly an Olympic sport. Some days she got back home and her face just ached, she'd smiled so much. She smiled at everyone in the playground, the teachers, everyone she passed on the pavement, people in the shops, those who served her, passing cyclists, dog walkers, the window cleaner, the fish van man, the lady who lived in the wonky house on the corner.

In fairness, a lot of people smiled back. But Thea had no idea who any of them actually were. And she longed for a proper face-to-face conversation with a real person. It was worst when she passed the coffee shop in the village. It always seemed to be full of laughter, women's faces creased in glee, others buried in deep conversation. The fabulous smell of fresh coffee wafted out as if it had cartoon arms of steam attempting to drag her in. The cakes in the window had that fresh baked glow, the scones the biggest she had ever seen.

Well, it was Devon, after all — the land of clotted cream, creamy rich butter and much of the best produce the country had to offer. It was partly why she and Derek had chosen to move to this charming village, tucked away on the outskirts of Dartmoor, history stroking the very chimney pots of the place.

"It really will be a new start love," Derek had assured her, "it's time to move on. And besides, Immy will love it. The school is a really good one and she'll make new friends. And we'll be able to carry our shopping home, no more supporting corporate greed at the supermarket — you can get that basket you've always wanted to fill up with local pork chops and home-made strawberry jam. It'll go great with all that bread you've been threatening to bake," he laughed.

It had been hard to resist the dream of such a rural idyll. So when Derek was offered a job in Exeter, a promotion with a sought-after company, there had been no turning back. Friends and family were appalled at their plan.

"After everything you've been through," said her sister.

"But it will make it so much harder for you," said her next door neighbour.

"Yes, and it will be a new start where no one will know," countered Derek. Thea had agreed. "We always planned to retire to Devon anyway," he said. "Now we'll get to enjoy so much more of it. And Immy will just love the beaches and we can explore Dartmoor. I'm told it's quite magical," smiled Derek, the biggest rock Thea had ever known.

Packing up their London life was a challenge on so many levels, pure joy on others. The thought of a better life for Immy kept Thea going, but she had never really thought through the realities of moving somewhere so different, somewhere they didn't know a soul. The move happened so quickly and here they were, three months down the line. Immy was settled in a wonderful new primary school, the cottage had come together beautifully and Derek kept saying he didn't know why they hadn't moved years ago.

He joined the local history group, played squash with new colleagues and bought them all walking boots. Immy was now in the Brownies and had learnt to swim. Thea felt lost and isolated, as if she were on the outside looking in. Walking past the coffee shop each school day morning had become inescapable torture. It felt like she had lost all her confidence and with autumn fast beckoning winter, she was terrified her own life was imploding.

***

Thea was so deep in her black treacle gloom she failed to see the woman waving at her from within the coffee shop. Just as she passed the second window she heard someone say "Hello there! Immy's mum isn't it?" Jolted out of her misery Thea turned to see the beaming round face of a large busted woman wearing ridiculously tight jeans. "Why don't you come and join us?"

Stunned into a temporary silence, Thea managed to smile — not quite Olympian standards, she was so surprised — and followed the woman inside.

"What are you having? Here we are. Sit yourself down. Move up Sam, make space."

"It's alright," smiled Sam, "Hannah is the bossy one. The rest of us just do what she says," and all the women laughed.

Bantering back Hannah grinned. "Well someone's got to organise you lot otherwise nothing would ever happen!"

"Yeah, yeah. Don't put Immy's mum off just yet, she looks like she might bolt at any second. By the way, what is your name?" enquired a pale skinned woman with curly blonde hair kinking out in all directions.

Regaining a modicum of composure Thea introduced herself before responding to the original question: "Oh, yes, please, I'll have a black coffee please. It always smells so good when I walk past," she blurted out, "thank you."

By the time she left the café Thea was sporting a grin worthy of a double gold. Just an hour in the company of a bunch of women was enough to pull her out of the gloom which had begun to descend on her life.

Hannah, who had beckoned her in, was clearly the clichéd, larger-than-life fog horn of the group, her warmth as evident as her embonpoint. Sam was tall, with an effortless glamour which dripped off her painted nails and be-ringed fingers. A single mum (did the men in the area have no taste, wondered Thea?) who ran her own marketing business. Then there was Jules, the blonde who turned out to be a potter. Lesley completed the group, as quiet as Hannah was loud. She made Thea feel so welcome by adding she too was a newcomer to Devon.

From what little she gleaned that morning — there was more laughing than talking — Thea was elated. With the promise of regular coffees she at last felt moving to Devon was going to work.

In the following weeks, Thea warmed to Hannah, Sam, Jules and Lesley, marvelling at what a diverse bunch of women they were. Sometimes they were joined by Susan, frequently stressed out by her full time career and four children. Hannah even persuaded Thea to join a local belly dancing club, as well as a pottery class run by Jules. But the more she felt a part of the group the more Thea began to feel uncomfortable.

"I'll have to tell them," she said to Derek one evening, "I feel like I'm being dishonest."

"Only you know if it's the right thing to do," smiled Derek, "I haven't told anyone at work; it just hasn't seemed relevant somehow."

"Yes, but it's different for women, isn't it? Women talk to each other far more about personal stuff; it's just the way it is. Sometimes a truth unsaid is like lying. They all seem like such an open, honest group of women."

A look of pain flashed across Derek's face, suddenly making him look so much older than his fifty eight years.

"We haven't done anything wrong, love. And not talking to other people about it doesn't make it any the less painful for me you know. If you want to tell them, then you must. And if they really are women who're going to be your friends then it's a risk you have to take. Trust your instincts."

It wasn't long before Thea had to make a decision. Hannah announced over a morning coffee they must all come for a girlie night at hers.

"It's time to swap caffeine for alcohol," she declared, "I'll do some nibbles. Sam, what about a babysitter? Shall I send Adrian round, he can fix that dripping tap for you at the same time?"

"Oh my hero," mocked Sam, fluttering her eyelashes, "besides, I know you want your hubby out of the house so you can let your hair down!"

"Sounds like a plan to me," grinned Hannah.

That Friday evening Thea was going to have to tell the truth. Maybe they would have to move again. It was too awful to contemplate. For the next two days she barely slept. She had to do the right thing, but it had to be the right thing for her — and for Derek and for Immy.

She knew she must trust her own instincts — and her instincts told her she was among a group of women who would understand. But what if she was wrong?

"Now go and have a good time, love," soothed Derek as Thea carefully placed a bottle of Merlot and a still warm batch of cheese straws in her hand-woven willow basket, bought recently at the Totnes country show. Derek still joked it had probably been crafted by fairies sitting on toadstools, even though they both knew it had been made by a yoga teacher who also offered classes on growing organic herbs and willow weaving.

"Just be you. This isn't London, Thea, people seem to have more time for each other down here. Come on girl — it's your first night out in Devon!"

With not far to walk, Thea relaxed as she strolled along a narrow cobbled street, the sun dipping behind the ancient rooftops, bathing slates and glinting off old glass as it slowly slipped behind the rolling hills framing the golden sky.

Knocking on Hannah's huge, peeling front door the big brass knocker lured Sam almost straight away.

"Come on in and join the party" smiled Sam, who wore an impossibly glamorous shift dress with pale grey leggings which almost shimmered. Thea was the last to arrive and what she saw almost took her breath away. One of the doors off the wide hallway led into a living room. The others — Hannah, Jules, Lesley and Susan — were ensconced within the friendly debris of a well used room, piles of magazines and papers competing for space amongst the assorted cabinets stuffed with old china and bric-a-brac, three miss-matched sofas, bright, soft-looking cushions, various chairs and footstools.

A cat sprawled across the back of the green sofa and, on what seemed like every available space, candles were burning, each throwing intoxicating shadows across wonky walls, recesses and intriguing looking objects which clearly showed Hannah had travelled widely. The whole effect was punctuated with glorious photographs of children, from babyhood to teenage years.

"Red or white?" asked Hannah, holding up a large, hand-blown wine glass.

"Oh, red please," breathed Thea, "here", she added, holding out the basket, "another for the collection — and I made us some cheese straws."

"Ooh, lovely!" squealed Jules, "my favourites."

Before she could stop herself Thea blurted out: "I love your living room!"

They all laughed before Susan said: "We all love Hannah's house, wait until you see the rest of it. It's a glorious hotchpotch of everything."

"I prefer to call it 'shabby chic'," smiled Hannah. The chatter round the room got louder as the wine levels in the bottles on the large oak coffee table fell. Talk of how they all came to be living in the same village turned the spotlight directly on Thea.

"So how come you ended up here?" It was a direct question from Lesley. Knowing she had no choice Thea took a deep breath.

"Actually, there's something I need to tell you all," she almost gulped. Her mouth was dry, her palms felt clammy and she knew she just had to get this over with. Even the candles seemed to dim as she began to speak. "I'm not actually Immy's mum. I'm her grandmother," whispered Thea.

For what seemed like minutes no one spoke. Lesley smiled at Thea and the understanding was evident: "We kind of thought so. We knew there was something, and that was one of the guesses."

"What, you've all been talking about me?" blurted out Thea, horrified. Hannah waded in:

"Of course love, you're a newcomer. But we don't talk to all the newbies — we're called 'blow ins' by the way."

"You feel an outcast when you first arrive, especially when you know you're a bit different," chimed in Sam.

"It's how we all got together really — Hannah was the first, but then she's been here forever." Hannah smiled at Sam, before turning back to Thea, who continued talking. "I knew I had to tell you all but I wasn't sure if anyone would understand and then I dithered for so long I felt like I'd been dishonest in not telling you in the first place. But," and Thea paused, took a large glug of wine, "it's a bit difficult really."

"We figured it probably was," prompted Hannah gently. With all eyes on her Thea tried to explain.

"My daughter lost her way. It's... well, it's complicated. She worked in the City, she did well, she started taking drugs and, well, it just all happened so quickly. She was vulnerable. She had an affair with a well-known banker. She fell pregnant. Days after Immy was born she went missing. The police were involved, it was all so awful."

Hannah refilled Thea's glass. "We still don't know if it was an accidental overdose, or suicide," Thea's face was etched with pain. "But we were eventually allowed to adopt Immy and, I suppose, Immy saved us both. She's why we're both still here. Andrea was our only child." She tailed off, afraid she was going to cry. Lesley silently re-filled everyone else's glasses as Hannah gave Thea a huge hug, tears in her eyes.

"You're in excellent company," she grinned. "All of us here have stories. It's why we get on. We've all experienced grief and pain and hardship and yet we are all still here – enjoying life." Wiping her eyes with a tissue proffered by Susan, Thea looked around the room.

"I left my husband for a woman," Lesley spoke first. "My children suffered most but they came round, in time."

"I fought breast cancer," Hannah kept up the momentum, "had to have a double mastectomy. The plastic surgeon refused to rebuild me as I had been. He came round though. I threatened to leave him if he didn't. I'm glad he changed his mind, I still adore him!"

Jules joined in: "I lost most my left arm in a car accident; they never caught the other driver. I had to give up my passion — I was a show jumper."

"She used to win medals," added Lesley.

"Ah, but back then I didn't know about pottery and now, my pots are my passion — along with the master potter I met at college. I'd rather have him in my life than I would my left arm!" It was all so much to take in, Thea sat in stunned silence.

"I guess I'm still looking for my silver lining," smiled Susan. "Two years ago, my husband was diagnosed with Motor Neurone Disease. It's hard, but the geneticists have told us all the children are clear, which is good news. And we take life where we can get it. We're a close family, with much family and friend support." Susan looked around the room. "These girls are my sanity," she laughed. "And we pack in so much. As a family we have travelled to so many places, seen so many things. It's why I work so much. We value our lives and we'll have so many memories for when it gets really tough."

"I just don't know what to say," mumbled Thea.

"It's OK," said Sam, "we kind of gravitated towards each other. This is not stuff you can pop into idle conversation over a quick coffee. It's hard for other mums, other villagers, to take it all on board. So we kind of stick together. We call ourselves the outcasts," laughed Sam.

"So what puts you on the outside?" blurted out Thea.

"Saving the best 'til last," laughed Hannah.

"I was born a man," said Sam.

Everyone roared with laughter at the look on Thea's face.

"But you're so beautiful," countered Thea.

"Why, thank you darling!" crooned Sam. "I was born with gender dysphoria, and my parents couldn't decide if I was girly enough to become one. They got it wrong, but it was a fifty-fifty gamble either way. I muddled along, feeling wrong and, by the time I hit my thirties I had a beautiful daughter of my own. Her mum couldn't cope with either of us, and I was left holding the baby. With my family and the NHS behind me, I went for it. My daughter has only ever known me as a woman, but she knows the truth and we're good. I wouldn't say I've found acceptance in deepest, darkest Devon," they all laughed as she continued, "but I have found contentment like I never thought possible. It also helps having this lot of misfits on board."

The glow around the room highlighted six faces. Six lives.

"I could get used to being an outcast," said Thea, not realising she'd said it out loud.

Chudleigh Phoenix Annual Short Story competition

Inspired by what you've read? Then visit www.chudleighphoenix.co.uk and see how you can have a go yourself.

By this time next year, you too could be in print.

By the same authors

Life is Not a Trifling Affair

By Elizabeth Ducie

Sunshine and Sausages

www.chudleighphoenix.co.uk